Bits of Me

Meghan Scott

ISBN-10:1502937867
ISBN-13:978-1502937865

DEDICATION

To my inspiration. I hope you know you who are.

ACKNOWLEDGMENTS

Thank you, thank you, thank you to my wonderful, clever, snarky friends who have kept me amused during this process and given me lines of dialogue from our very own conversations. You've read, encouraged, suggested and edited. You've supplied wine, food and laughter. You all know who you are. I love each and every one of you and am so lucky to have you in my life.

To all participants in equestrian sports, hats off to you, and my apologies for any liberties taken with your particular discipline. If I've glossed over, understated or exaggerated, please know that I know better and forgive me my transgressions in the interest of a better story.

1

I lay in the bed in my best friend's guest room, now my room, luxuriating in a late morning, the sun peeking in behind the white sheers and light blue draperies that framed the window. I closed my eyes again trying to capture the essence of my dream, not quite awake but still reluctant to leave my delicious dream guy. He was your typical tall dark and handsome, but the way he'd held me was tantalizing. I wanted to feel that forever, never waking up – or reach for my vibrator – either would work.

Damn! What was that?

The next round of knocking at my door made me jump a little. *Shit. How long had that been going on?* I leaped up, ran a brush partway through my auburn hair, at least until it snagged, tugged on an old t-shirt, and wiped the remnants of sleep from my eyes. More persistent knocking let me know this person was not going away anytime soon. *Gah!* I wiped some toothpaste quickly over my teeth with one finger.

"Coming!" I yelled.

I peeked out the window to see who it was and opened the door. Without hesitation, Sara bounced in, all golden waves and Chanel No. 5.

"There it is!" Sara said, grabbing her clutch from the counter. "I knew I'd left this here last night. Hey, did I wake you? God, I'm so thoughtless sometimes!"

I wondered if she could tell what I'd been dreaming about. I still wasn't down from that sexual high yet and was a little embarrassed; as if I'd been caught doing something wicked. *It could have been wicked if I hadn't been interrupted.* I didn't know her that well yet. She was my roommate's neighbor and good friend.

"Well it is after nine, so you've every right to think everyone would be up," I laughed, hoping she wouldn't notice my embarrassment. "I guess I'm not acclimated to the time zone yet. I was up late sorting through all my stuff before my meeting at the magazine. Amy's already gone off to work but she's determined to drag me to some party tonight - in honor of my arrival - she says. I'm looking forward to the party actually," I admitted. "It will be good to get out and meet people and maybe make a few contacts."

Sara perched herself on a barstool. "So – ummm - I'm sorry I skipped out on you guys last night. It's just – well – when Steve called and got off work early – ah - you know." She blushed and I laughed.

Steve was her young veterinarian fiancé, fresh out of school. He had just started working with one of the major veterinary hospitals in Lexington. The vets worked long hours and sometimes into the night, never knowing when they might be called out in the wee hours of the morning, so I understood where Sara was coming from. They were young and in love. Sara had just finished her student teaching and had secured a job, starting in the fall, at one of the prestigious private elementary schools in our part of town. Well, Amy and Sara's part of town, anyway. I hadn't been there long enough to claim it as mine yet.

"Hey – no problem. I know how young love can be – romance and all that. So are ya'll going to the big shindig at the Horse Park tonight?"

"Oh I wouldn't miss it!" she gushed. "My family's been involved for years and it raises so much money for charity. My mother's on the board – so it's a given I have to go. I bet you didn't know it's the one event that includes every breed, every discipline – from dressage, working western, and racing – you name it – and everyone comes together this one night just for charity. I just hope Steve doesn't get called away on a farm call. He's gonna look so sexy in a tux, the thought makes me drool!"

"Whoa, girl! Don't make us man-less bitches jealous this early in the morning!" I teased as we walked to the door. If only she knew what I'd been dreaming about. "See ya there!"

Young love. I shook my head. Amy and I were only five years older than Steve and Sara, but it was a world of difference at this stage. And I lied about knowing what all that romance stuff was about. I'd had boyfriends and I was certainly no virgin. But the mind blowing sex and soul stirring love of novels and chick flicks? Never happened for me. I didn't really see what the fuss was about. In high school and college, it was just so much overactive hormones, experimentation and sticky groping in the dark. Not that I hated sex. It could be pleasant sometimes. But I'd never had an orgasm that didn't involve batteries.

I had high hopes when I moved to New York, taking a position at a major ad agency. I was naïve about a few things then. First, I thought I'd make tons of money. That one was true actually, except rent ate most of it. Second, I thought some debonair New York billionaire would sweep me off my feet and we'd fall madly in love and have amazing sex. But all I found there were assholes, paying for dinner and expecting something in return. Really – it'd have been cheaper if they'd hired a call girl. They were all about themselves and their careers. If you didn't sleep with them, you were bored to tears, and if you did, you were probably still bored to tears. Then they never called. I was just done with it. It was much more fun to flirt outrageously, watch them act the fool, and then leave. I'd been called a tease. I didn't care.

Then I actually thought I found a good one, but I wasted a year on him, and even moved in with him, only to discover he wanted to dictate what I wore, how I did my hair and even what car I drove. How I didn't see those warning signs, I will never know. I tried to please him for a while, the whole female 'ticking time clock' of fertility pestering my psyche. But I woke up one day, realized that thirty wasn't ancient, looked at him ranting and raving over some imagined slight and thought, *"Who the fuck do you think you are?"* I wasn't raised to be subservient to some man who needed his ego stroked. I packed my bags and left. I called my best friend Amy from the road to tell her I was on my way. My professional reputation was probably in the gutter over that one. I remembered to call my boss halfway to Kentucky.

I stepped outside, collecting the paper and mail. The sun was shining and Amy's perfectly manicured lawn was a deep green. The air smelled fresh somehow – less noise and definitely less pollution. After being in New York for five years, it was a refreshing change, even if I did miss the hustle and bustle, the great clubs, and fantastic theater. I wondered what my parents would have thought of my rash behavior.

A drunk driver killed them, not three blocks from my childhood home in Akron, Ohio, shortly after I moved to New York. I went home for a few weeks to put things in order. It was all my firm would allow. The sorrow and rage still hit me sometimes, especially when I needed advice or just thought of something funny they would have liked and realized I couldn't call home anymore. I'd boxed up the house, donated some things and kept others in storage. Emotionally unable to sell the house, I'd leased it to an older couple who wanted to be near their grandchildren.

I set the mail on the kitchen counter, grabbed a Diet Coke from the fridge and flipped through the paper. I rinsed the dishes in the sink and put them in the dishwasher, careful to hold the door. A spring was broken and the door crashed with a loud bang if we didn't hold it. I made a mental note to call a repairman. Amy would never remember.

Amy's house wasn't huge, but it was a comfortable, well-built older home. The pool was a bonus, and Amy loved to entertain. On any given night, people were dropping by for an hour or two to sit by the pool and have a glass of wine. Eventually, I would need to get my own place. Of course, Amy said I could stay as long as I liked. She had been my best friend since high school and we had roomed together all through college. We'd shared the good, the bad, and the ugly and still finished each other's sentences. Even after college, when we'd gone separate ways, we texted daily. She had dropped everything to lend a hand when my parents died.

Amy, with her bright red hair, was spontaneous and ambitious and she liked her wine and her martinis. She'd been married once, for about a year, to a real bastard whom she subsequently dumped. She started her own insurance firm in Lexington and had satellite offices in Louisville and other cities. She primarily insured racehorses, but another division of her firm insured show horses. We had grown up showing saddle seat horses together, training out of the same barn, though she rode Saddlebreds and I had primarily Arabs and Half-Arabs.

I glanced at the clock on the microwave, noting I had a few hours before meeting the staff at *Kentucky Equine* magazine, the local voice of the horse industry. As luck would have it they were looking for a new marketing director, and Amy, who knew everyone, had suggested me. The magazine was the oldest of its kind in Kentucky, but newer, fresher magazines had cut into the market. *Kentucky Equine* still relied on old standby advertisers and subscribers. The articles had gone stale and the magazine was on the decline. A few local horsemen had bought the magazine and were trying to bring it back to life but had no clue what they were doing. I was actually excited about it. I got to bring my journalism degree and advertising experience to an industry I loved.

I debated a suit versus a more casual dress and decided slower paced Kentucky on a summer day warranted the dress and a pair of Coach wedge sandals. I poured some coffee into my travel mug, grabbed my laptop, my purse and my satchel and left the house.

The current small staff of *Kentucky Equine* was fantastic and welcoming. They were excited to try fresh ideas, and I told them I wanted everyone, even interns, to feel free to voice opinions. I wanted an invigorating atmosphere that welcomed creativity at all levels. We met in the conference room and I laid out in more detail, some of my ideas, and encouraged each member to think outside the box.

Through my work in New York, I was thoroughly versed in all phases of advertising and marketing, but there I had teams of support staff for every aspect and I mainly pitched ideas to clients. Sometimes, I delegated the pitch, too, depending on the account. The *Kentucky Equine*, however, was going to require more hands-on involvement, and I was excited to get back to my journalism roots. They also loved my idea of starting a branch service of event planning. The open houses or parties would go hand-in-hand with feature articles and spreads on advertisers. It would mean more exposure for the magazine and more revenue as well. Plus, it was a service no other magazine was doing.

As it was Friday, assignments for those covering social events were handed out. Pretty much the entire staff was going to the Horse Park for the charity event. I told them this was a great opportunity to gather new ideas for articles, gain new advertisers, and pitch the new event planning service. We were also going to pitch huge advertising spreads on heavier stock with accompanying write-ups and interviews. I learned that one of our interns was a computer guru, and set her to working on taking the magazine online, something we were terribly behind the curve on. I left the meeting feeling thoroughly energized.

2

Amy came in at 4:30, a whirlwind with red curls. "I took off early! And I gave everyone else the rest of the day too – as long as they donated! So I already have a pot of cash to take tonight. Now – let's have a glass of wine and discuss your wardrobe!"

"Hello to you too, Amy!" I said sarcastically. "How about 'how did your meeting go?' Geez, all you care about is how I look – you don't give a shit about my brain," I fake pouted, making fun of my ex.

"You know it, girlfriend!" she laughed. Then she sighed heavily and rolled her eyes. "Ok – how was your meeting? As if I didn't already know. I mean, I offered them a true blue fresh from New York advertising executive and delivered her straight up with an olive."

"Amy!" I acted shocked. "I am NOT a martini! And that doesn't make any sense anyway! But it did go well. So I guess I owe you thanks for the introduction. You single handedly saved me from my spontaneous decision to abdicate my throne at the agency. They didn't even question my sudden appearance in Kentucky. Guessing you left the 'she didn't even give notice' part out?"

Amy screwed her mouth in a funny twist and rolled her

eyes. On a more serious note I added, "Honestly, I thought I'd be living off savings for a few months. So really, I do owe you one."

"Nope. You don't. It's what best friends do. And let's face it - you're great at what you do. They feel lucky to have you. And, I already heard through the grapevine that they love your idea of adding some event planning into the marketing structure. Great move, there."

"Thanks," I told her. "It's something I've wanted to try. And I figured it might be a good fit."

"Right. Speaking of fit, let's get back to that hair and wardrobe bit."

I groaned. "Ugh! You rhymed! Go easy on me Amy – you know flamboyant isn't my thing. I'm going for tasteful here – and I'm hoping to do some networking to build my clientele – I don't think slutty is going to cut it."

"Depends on what clientele you're after!"

"Oh!" I threw my towel at her. "You're horrid and bitchy and witchy and I've no idea why we're friends!"

"It's why you love me, honey – you need someone to live vicariously through. But I swear – you could use a little – um – release if you know what I mean. Really. How long has it been since you've had an orgasm that didn't involve your vibrator and a romance novel?"

"Oh my god, Amy – shut up! Too long." Maybe never – nothing earth shattering anyway. "I may well qualify as a virgin. But I don't care. I'm holding out for nonexistent Mr. Right at this point."

"Well – fine – at least when I'm done with you, every man in the place will be weak in the knees – they'll chase you all over the place and you can flirt your ass off and then disappear – one of these days though, some prince is gonna find the high heel that fits and that Cinderella act is gonna be over."

I started giggling. "The high heel? Really? More like the muck boot…now that'd be a sight!"

"Oh – yes! And some grungy nails and stained jeans

and Walmart friggin underwear and…" She interrupted her monologue and tipped the wine bottle. "Oh here – you need more wine!"

We were giggling so hard I had to sit down on the bathroom floor and Amy was using the wall as support. The thought of waltzing into a gala evening looking like field hands just to shock the Grande Dames of Kentucky and beyond was evil even for us. We'd been known for such pranks in our college years. Amy was still mostly irreverent. I respected the hell out of her for saying exactly what she thought when she thought it and to and about whom she thought it about. The girl had balls, that's for sure.

She brought out an exquisite black dress, the bodice of which had a deep V neckline edged with satin. Satin ribbon spaghetti straps enhanced with rhinestones dropped from the shoulders to criss cross under my breasts and continued to tie in the back. The fitted waist gave way to several layers of lightest chiffon – it was the perfect cross of sexy and classy. Matching kitten heels completed the outfit.

"Amy it's perfect!"

"And you didn't trust me," she chided.

I pulled my hair up in a loose chignon with tendrils of auburn hair escaping and secured it with sparkling pins.

Amy donned a stunning strapless red dress that gathered and wrapped in such a way as to cover everything and still leave nothing to the imagination. Yup. She was daring like that.

"Wow." I admired her.

"Well – wow yourself. Let's go get'em killer!"

We giggled like school girls and headed for the door.

"Holy fantasy land!" I exclaimed when I saw the park.

"You're going to catch bugs if you don't shut your mouth," Amy laughed. "But yeah, what they do to this place for the party is nothing short of amazing."

The Kentucky Horse Park, for the uninitiated, was spectacular at any time. It included rows of white barns with green roofs, paved walkways, green pastures, and miles of white fences stretching to infinity. The park boasted statues of some of the most famous horses that ever lived, immortalized forever in bronze in various gardens. The Park was home to several major breed and discipline headquarters as well as The Museum of the Horse and the new Arabian Horse Galleries. There were the famous cross-country course, the many dressage rings, the hunter jumper rings and the two coliseums that hosted all manner of equestrian sports.

But tonight – tonight it was transformed by an endless sea of open-air tents draped with billowing yards of gauzy white fabric and temporary pavilions with real doors and windows. Crystal chandeliers hung from the ceilings and candles flickered on every table. Miniature lights outlined everything from the tents and pavilions to the surrounding trees. The effect was ethereal. You couldn't help but believe in fantasies in a place like this.

"You go ahead Amy – I'm staying right here. My prince will be riding up at any minute on his white horse to whisk me away."

"Yeah – it's beautiful. But know this…" and she narrowed her eyes and lifted her lips in a tiny smirk, "The real magic happens between the sheets. And if you're lucky, the horse isn't the only thing that prince will be riding."

"Oh jeez Amy, you slut– way to kill my romantic fantasy!"

She nudged me with her elbow and winked, "Hey mine's a better fantasy and you know it. Except mine doesn't have to be fantasy! However, we have to get down there to make it come true. Let's go check in and find the nearest bar. We'll rub elbows a little and find the dance floor!"

"Sounds like a plan, girlfriend."

At the welcome tent, we handed our tickets to a couple of enthusiastic volunteers, who handed out maps.

"It's like an amusement park!" I was in awe. Amy grinned and pointed out the tents with different foods, bars, jazz bands, string quartets and tables for seating. A dance floor with a DJ was set up under a grove of trees. Each area was sponsored by a different organization. Several thousand people were expected. "Seriously, Amy, this is incredible. I can't believe all these people came together to put this on. I can't even think straight right now!"

"Well let's start by grabbing food, hit up a bar and see who we see." She dragged me over to a food tent. We piled our plates with everything from salmon to pasta salad, took glasses of an excellent Merlot from a wandering server and nabbed a table where we could people watch.

"So," continued Amy, "I say we end up the night at the dance floor. Oh I know you want to network, and that's great, but surely you can find some guy that interests you enough to at least dance with."

"Amy, you have a one-track mind," I laughed.

I scanned the room and beyond, taking in the men in tuxedos and ladies in evening gowns, some simple and some obviously couture. A sea of people moved around. I noticed groups laughing or talking seriously, trainers talking to riders, agents making contacts, deals being struck, and groups of owners glorying in the day's results of various shows taking place on the grounds.

Stable workers in the distance were doing chores, watering, feeding, and cleaning tack and closing up for the night - shadows moving in the lights of the barns. Farther, horses worked in an arena – some late night schooling for horses to be shown first thing in the morning. During breaks in the music from the bands, neighs were carried on the wind.

Amy punched me in the arm. "Hey! Earth to Mel! Look, isn't that Nancy Obermeyer? Holy shit, I haven't her since we were kids!"

"You know? I think you're right. I thought she was the coolest grown-up ever! Nancy was like a second mom to me, you know? I can't believe we lost touch." Nancy was one of those larger-than-life personalities and we had idolized her. She'd also had a string of champion show horses and the money to promote them. But she always encouraged us as young riders. She'd even listened to our adolescent worries and treated us to wild rides in her convertible BMW. Oh how we'd loved her.

"Let's go say hi before she disappears in this throng!"

We made our way to where we'd last seen Nancy, swiping another glass of Merlot off a table on the way.

"Nancy?" I tapped her on the shoulder.

"Well, I'll be!" Nancy exclaimed. "Melanie? Amy? Is that you? Oh my god – it's been ages! I've thought about you girls for years!" She put a hand on Amy's arm. "If I'm being honest, Amy, I knew you were in Kentucky. Our paths just haven't crossed and that's my fault. But now you're both here!"

She hugged me and turned to her friends, "Last time I saw this one, she was headed to New York to be a hotshot ad-woman. What the heck you doing in these parts?" she asked me.

"I decided it was time for a change of scenery. I'm hopefully here permanently. I'm the new marketing director for *Kentucky Equine*. I'm staying with Amy until I can get my own place. What in the world are you doing these days?"

"I moved down here a few years ago. When I cut back on my showing, I wanted to stay involved, so I took up managing horse shows and I really enjoy it. I get to see everyone I know, meet new people, and give back to my show community. I've even started travelling to manage shows in other states."

"Nancy, that's fantastic! I bet you're great. I have no doubt you're in great demand."

"I can't believe it. Ya'll are all grown up, my god. That's it! We are definitely getting together to stir up some trouble around here!"

"Nancy you always keep things stirred," said a nice looking older man next to her. He winked at me, "Don't let her tell you otherwise – she is trouble with a capital 'T'. And don't argue with her – she's never wrong!"

Clearly an inside joke between the two of them.

"Abe– I was only wrong once – and I divorced his ass."

I almost spit up my wine.

"Humph. You've been wrong one more time, my feisty friend." Abe grinned slyly. "You won't go out with me."

Nancy gave him a peck on the cheek. "But you know I secretly adore you, Abe."

"One of these days, Nance," he retorted.

This was obviously an on-going thing I didn't fully understand. I stood there grinning stupidly. I'd obviously missed a lot of Nancy's life.

"Abe, hon, these girls don't know about my ex. Hell, not too much to tell." She rolled her eyes and looked at me. "He wanted a quiet life and lots of kids. I can't have any so one day he just packed his bags and moved in with a more fertile version of me."

"Good god – that's awful!" Amy gasped.

"Eh – it's fine now. It's truly for the best. He was nice guy. He just wanted different things. His oldest daughter just started riding, imagine that, so I have to run into them sometimes."

"So you're still showing?" I asked.

"I've slowed down a bit, but," she leaned in conspiratorially, "I've picked up a new discipline! I'm learning to jump!"

I just shook my head and smiled. Same Nancy I

remembered. She had to be in her sixties now, not that she'd admit it. I loved her spunk.

"And I still have George, of course. He's retired now after six Five-Gaited World Championships."

"Yeah – sure! I used to love to watch you on him."

"I'm planning to stand him at stud." She paused for a minute. "Marketing director, huh. I'm going to need an ad campaign for George – maybe we could meet and discuss?"

"Wow, sure! I'd love to work on your project! Tell you what - I'm sure I have some time next week. I could swing by your barn and start going over some stuff. But I'd also like to catch up with you personally. It's been a long time."

Maybe coming to this party was going to be lucrative after all. Amy excused herself to the bathroom leaving me to attend to more wine. Not seeing a waiter, I made my way to the bar, making small talk with a few people standing in line. I turned to put my empty glass down and that's when I saw him.

Or felt, rather than saw – because I swear the heat from his eyes burned right through me. Prickles of desire spread through my body as if he had touched me from across the room. He was the hottest guy I'd ever seen; the kind that graces the covers of romance novels and causes married women to look askance at their husbands. His sun kissed tan set off full sultry lips and perfect white teeth. His thick dark hair fell over one eye giving him a dangerous air as he conversed with a crowd of women who were hanging on his every word. Instead of formal attire, he wore a white dress shirt, unbuttoned at the neck, jeans and a sport coat. He was the most gorgeous man I'd ever seen. *He's just another man, Mel. Leave it.*

Only my body said otherwise. The way that denim hugged his ass and thighs was nothing short of sinful. Broad shoulders and muscular chest tapered down to a fine waist and I imagined running my hands over those abs. *Stop it.* I was ogling and I knew it. *No harm in looking, right?*

I chanced a glance at his face again. *Shit.* He caught me looking. His sensual mouth curved slightly in a knowing grin and he cocked his head imperceptibly. His eyes never left mine, even as he nodded and smiled, acknowledging the expensive looking women surrounding him. He locked me in his gaze, unable to move, and I swear he knew what I looked like under my dress. I wondered what it would feel like to have those arms wrapped around me, his body having its way with mine. *Fuck! What the hell was I doing?* I realized I'd been standing there too long when he suddenly winked at me and turned away. Released from his penetrating stare, I took a breath. Never had any man had this effect on me, and I didn't even know him. I didn't want to. He was far too dangerous.

"Ahem…" the bartender got my attention. *Crap.* People were waiting. "Two Merlots, please." I took the glasses and stepped away to wait for Amy. I couldn't help but steal another glance in Mr. Tall Dark and Dangerous' direction. He was looking right at me and his intense scrutiny left no doubt what he was thinking. I had to get out of there.

"See something you like?" Amy reappeared none too soon. "You're practically drooling, dear. Someone getting your panties wet?"

"Amy! You're disgusting!" I laughed, relieved at the break in tension. "I got caught ogling. I'm mortified and we need to go dance. Now!"

She stole a look in the direction I'd been staring. "Oh. I see. Hmmmm…well. Wouldn't you rather dance with him? He looks like he'd like to do more than that. He's still checking you out."

"Amy, we are leaving," I warned, knowing she'd likely embarrass me by dragging my ass over there and saying something inappropriate. I marched out of the tent toward the dance floor.

"Hey, slow down! Heels aren't made for running!" Amy giggled.

The dance floor covered an entire outdoor arena. Colored spotlights hung in the trees highlighting the DJ and mass of writhing bodies. Amy and I stood at the low fence watching while we finished our wine.

"So, do you know him?" I asked.

"Ah. You *are* interested!" she teased. "Contrary to popular belief, I don't know everyone. He's not one of my clients. But if *you* aren't interested, I'd *love* to handle his account."

"Amy, you are incorrigible. You make business sound pornographic. I'm not handling his anything. Let's dance."

The wine had gone to my head and I felt the flush of warmth loosen my joints as we danced to some top 40 hits and some good oldies, singing along with the ones we knew. A couple of guys joined us for a while and were probably disappointed when we declined their invitation to leave. The DJ, catering to the young crowd, played the latest techno craze. The insistent beat of *Animals* was intoxicating. I closed my eyes and let my body feel the music, the hard driving beat dictating the dance. I felt hands on my hips and a rock hard body pressed against my backside. My head tilted back as I leaned into the pressure. *Too. Much. Wine. Unprofessional.* I tried to straighten, but the hands held me close. Hot breath nuzzled my ear and sent delicious shivers down my spine.

"I thought you'd disappeared."

I froze. *Shit.* It was Mr. Dangerous. I didn't have to look to know. I searched around quickly trying to find Amy, but she was across the floor. She saw me and waved innocently. *Bitch.*

"Do you taste as good as you smell?" From any other man, that might have been creepy, but this guy made me want to rip my clothes off right there on the dance floor.

What the fuck?

I didn't even have a smartass comeback. "I, umm, need to get a drink."

I broke his hold, pushed through the sea of people and wandered out under the trees. A slight breeze had picked up, catching the lights in the leaves and making them twinkle. I stood for a minute to catch my breath and take in the peaceful surroundings. What had just happened in there?

"So. Do you make a habit of flirting with men and then running off?"

My heart jumped and my wine sloshed over the edge of my glass. He was right there – I could feel the heat blazing off him. My knees went weak and I wasn't sure I could take another step if I wanted to. I slowly backed up and leaned on the tree behind me for support.

He came closer, placing one arm over my shoulder against the tree. I stared at his biceps, my body betraying the yearning I felt. His smoldering eyes were dark with desire, dangerous, predatory, animal.

"I umm - no, I don't. I mean, huh?" I'd forgotten his question already. *Think, Mel.* "Do you stalk people often?"

"Didn't mean to startle you," he smiled in amusement, "but you certainly jumped. You seem a little uneasy. I don't bite. I promise.

"What – you're not a vampire?" *What? Was I stupid? Idiot.*

"Not last time I checked. But I do appreciate beauty when I see it – and if I'm not mistaken, you don't dislike what you see. You feel it too."

Holy shit – what the hell? Who was this guy? Maybe it was the wine, but I couldn't help myself. I just stood there stupidly, hoping he would kiss me. His free hand explored my neck, traced my jaw, and turned my face up to meet his. The charge in the air around us was palpable. I took in the scent of him, masculine and strong. I felt a flush of heat on my skin as I stared at his mouth lowering to claim mine. Intense electrical pulses exploded through me and I was lost.

His sensuous lips were soft but forceful, taking what they needed and creating a carnal ache within me that I didn't understand. His hand caressed my face and he deepened the kiss, his body towering over mine. I felt his heart beat through his shirt as his tongue met mine - swirling, coaxing, devouring. His teeth nipped my lower lip, and his mouth tasted a trail along my throat, my neck, and down to the sensitive skin between the swells of my aching breasts. *Yes.* My body responded in a way it never had with any man – ever.

He brought his face back up to mine and hungrily took my mouth again, demanding everything I had. One hand slipped down behind my waist, pulling me into him. The other traced the curve of my breasts, teasing my nipples through my dress. My thighs clenched to hold back the throbbing ache between my legs. He spread me with his knees and crushed me into him. I felt him hard through the material of his jeans and my dress - the slight friction igniting my throbbing sex and sending shockwaves through my body. My hands clenched in his hair as I came from just his kiss, using his body to support my trembling legs, wanting him and not caring who might see – this total hot stranger…

What the hell – stranger – what was I doing? I came to my senses and broke the kiss wrenching myself away.

"I uh – what the fuck!" I panted hoarsely, more to myself than to him. I forced myself to break his gaze. He seemed amused or at least pleased with himself.

"Asshole," I whispered, angry, confused and embarrassed by my response to him. "I uh – I gotta go find someone." I wasn't making any sense. I needed air. *Did I really just have an orgasm? From a kiss?*

I turned and fairly ran, as best as possible in heels, down to the dance tent to find Amy.

What had I just done? I didn't even know his name! My mind was racing, torn between replaying the heated exchange of a moment before, and suffering from the realization of what'd I'd engaged in with a total stranger. *Cool off. Think.* If I never saw him again, no harm no foul. But Jesus – what if he was a potential client or worse, the husband of a potential client? My reputation was going to be in shambles. It was not professional and not how I wanted to start this new life of mine. Letting some guy have his way with me under the trees? Behaving so wantonly? But the fire he'd ignited was still burning. *What the hell was that?* As much as I hated to admit it, I had wanted him as much as he seemed to want me. I knew I had too much to drink already, but I needed another glass of wine.

I was just calming down when I saw Amy headed my way. "Where the hell did you disappear to?" she asked gaily, unaware of my discomfort.

I smoothed my dress down quickly and tucked stray wisps of hair into my wrecked chignon.

"Give up, honey," Amy laughed. "There's no fixing that 'do'. That looks like well fucked bedhead to me, but since that's not possible, I suggest staying away from the dance floor."

I hoped I didn't look as guilty as I felt. As much as I loved Amy, I wasn't ready to tell her about my encounter. I wasn't sure I understood it myself. I gave up on the chignon, removed the pins, and shook out my long hair, wavy from being pinned up. It would have to do.

"I'm about ready to head home I think," I hinted to Amy.

"Well, I'm starving. So let me get a bite to eat, say a few goodbyes, and we can head out. My feet are killing me anyway. You'd think with all these people, I'd find at least one interesting man – at least one that isn't taken or gay." She sighed and I chuckled at her. One day, some guy was going to knock her for a loop and she was going to eat all her smartass comments.

I figured while Amy was stuffing her face again, I better get some water or I was going to have a massive hangover. Probably would anyway, but it wouldn't hurt to rehydrate myself starting now. I felt a light touch at my elbow. I tensed, on guard now for temptations, but it was Abe, Nancy's friend.

"I was about to go, but I wanted to say I was most pleased to meet you and I think you're just what *Kentucky Equine* needs. And," he said, "I'd like to discuss business with you. I own a thoroughbred farm not too far outside of town."

"I'd be delighted," I said, smiling at him. He had kind features and I warmed to him instantly. He was the kind of man a girl instantly trusts. He reminded me of my father.

He reached out and tapped someone on the back. "Jake, boy, turn around here. I'd like to introduce you to someone."

I wanted to crawl in a hole right then and there. Jake, *so that was his name*, turned and favored me with the most dazzling smile. My face was aflame and I just hoped no one noticed.

As Abe made the introduction, Jake took my hand in his and smirked at me.

"So nice to meet you, Melanie, was it?"

"Yes," I managed to answer without squawking. "Nice to meet you too, Jake." I regained my composure and met his gaze straight on, not giving an inch to his glittering eyes.

If Abe noticed the tension, he didn't let on. He chattered happily away explaining that Jake was a highly respected hunter/jumper trainer.

"And Mel, here. She hails from a big New York City agency. She's going to revamp the *Kentucky Equine* and start event planning as a sideline of the magazine's service."

"Is that so?" Jake replied. He wouldn't let go of my hand. He shifted to position himself next to me and laced his fingers through mine. The sensation was distracting and thrilling. The nerve endings of my fingers sparked at each point of contact. I inwardly cringed, wanting to yank my hand away and go bury my head somewhere. I couldn't free myself without risking detection by Abe.

Each time I politely tried to slip my hand away, Jake tightened his hold and began caressing my palm with his thumb. *What are you doing to me?* I glared at him, but he just smiled as if making casual conversation with women he'd just made out with but never met was the most natural thing in the world. I wanted to kill him. I wanted to fuck him.

"And do you ride as well as you dance?" he asked, eyes dancing, making a wicked insinuation. "I think I noticed you and your friend on the dance floor," he added, mostly for Abe's benefit.

"I used to. Currently horse-less." I shrugged. *You can let me go now.* I lifted an eyebrow at him. *Take the hint.* Oh, he took the hint all right, but he wasn't giving in.

"Well steer clear of Buddy Olsen then if you don't want a new one," laughed Abe. "He'll fix that. He's been making the rounds heavy tonight." He explained that Buddy was a well-known agent. He was honest, as far as horse traders went, and could find the perfect match for any rider in any breed. But if an unsuspecting soul even hinted at wanting a horse, they were parting with their money in short order, and a new horse was in the barn. Buddy was very good at his job.

"In fact, there he is now. If you kids will excuse me, I actually have business with him." Abe took his leave of us, leaving us alone to face each other.

Awkward.

"Is your friend still here or can I see you home?" Jake asked. I didn't see Amy, and I was ready to kill her for disappearing, but she wouldn't leave without telling me.

"I think I'm good, thanks." I told him, looking for any way to escape.

He leaned close and whispered gruffly in my ear, "I imagine you are."

My stomach twisted in knots at the heated suggestion. I wanted this man. I could take him home and let him ravish me in ways I probably hadn't thought of. I was seriously even considering it. I could blame it on the wine later, I argued with myself.

"Oh Jaaaaake – ahhh - there you are Hon." A tall leggy honey-blond girl fairly stumbled into him, completely trashed. She appeared to be in her late twenties, dressed in a shockingly short mini dress, with a low enough neckline that her ample breasts nearly spilled out. She slipped her arm thru Jakes possessively and tossed her golden hair back. She held onto him for balance as she leaned to slip first one and then the other shoe off her feet. "Darling, my feet are killing me. I have got to get out of here. Be a love and give me a ride, will ya?" She batted her eyelashes at him. "Oh and I've got a lovely little bar for a nightcap for your trouble."

Unbelievable. I was such a fool. Better to find out now, though, before I actually considered taking him home.

Finally, she noticed me standing there. "Oh hi," she said, eyeing me up and down. She drunkenly stuck out a hand to shake mine, but it threw her off balance and the hand ended up on Jake's chest. Something twisted inside me. *Was I jealous? I barely knew the guy!* The blond weaved a little and giggled. "I'm Pam Bartlett – are you a new client of Jake's? He's *sooo* good. And *I* should know." I didn't think she was talking about horses now and I was pretty sure she wasn't talking to me.

I yanked my hand and this time, Jake let me go. Guys were all the same. But cheating on his girlfriend when she was at the same party? That was as low as it got.

"So nice to meet you both," I snarked. I made my exit as quickly and gracefully as I could.

"Amy, you bitch, what the hell? You were supposed to get some food and be right back!" I scolded her when I found her entertaining herself by flirting with some younger men.

"Oh, I know. But you were all tied up with Mr. Hunky over there."

"Well, his girlfriend showed up so that's out of the question. Can we get out of here now?"

Amy strained her neck to get a look at the girlfriend. "Oh my god. Really? He's dating her? Wow – there's just no accounting for taste, I guess."

"Why? You know her?"

"Only by reputation. Total ho. Brainless bimbo. She's fucked her way through most of the trainers in Kentucky is what I heard. In fact, I hear she takes her panties off to keep the flies off her face!"

"AMY! That's the most disgusting thing you've said all night!"

She smiled sweetly. "I know. It's why you love me! Now – let's go home and I have to tell you about the guy I just met!"

I should have known what was keeping her so long. I rolled my eyes. But the way she talked about this one, I thought he might actually have a chance.

Back at the house, Amy let herself into my bathroom and plopped herself on the floor while I brushed my teeth.

"Hell of a party, yeah?"

"Ummmmm-hmmmm," I mumbled, trying to avoid drooling toothpaste foam.

"So, you had the hots for that guy, Jake was it? The dreamy one with the nice ass?"

"And the girlfriend, don't forget. Do we have to talk about me? You know I'm not interested in dating anyway. I don't need a man. I do just fine alone. Men just complicate things and then fuck it all up. Anyway, it appears he's into dating boobs, not brains, right? You mentioned something about a guy you met? One of the sweet young things? Are all his tattoos at least symmetrical?"

"Ha. Ha. Very funny." She rolled her eyes at me. "No. This one's the serious type. Nice, actually. Hush – I know what you're going to say. Don't get me wrong, he's flippin hot! But he's kind and studious and for some reason, that turns me on. Maybe I'm growing up?"

We looked at each other and broke into giggles.

"Naaaah!" we laughed in unison.

"No but seriously, Mel. He's an attorney with Anderson & Scott and concentrates his practice on equine law, so he gets us. Not like people who just don't understand. Horse people are kind of a different breed, so to speak. And he asked me on a real date. Dinner. Oh my."

This was different. Amy was really into this guy. For her sake, I hoped he was everything she thought he was. She was such an awesome girl but her direct manner intimidated a lot of guys. She acted as if it didn't bother her and covered up her hurt with outrageous flirtations. To her credit, she had never changed herself for any man. She lived life on her own terms. I admired her. I had learned the hard way that twisting yourself inside out to please a guy never ended well. It was better, if lonelier, to be true to yourself.

Amy excused herself to her room. I climbed in my own bed and wondered if I would dream about fantasy guy tonight. Dream guy never had a bimbo on his arm.

3

I got up before the alarm, awakened by the automatic coffee maker percolating in the other room. I padded to the bathroom, thinking I was still tired from the party. We were probably much too old for such shenanigans. It took a week to recover. Thank goodness we'd done nothing but sit by the pool all weekend to nurse our hangovers. Sara had joined us. She told us Steve had been called for a colic during the party, and they had to leave early. That explained why we hadn't seen them, but at least they'd been able to go for a little while. We read magazines, drank iced tea and napped on rafts. I tried to put thoughts of Jake behind me. I had things to accomplish that didn't include embarrassing myself.

The office was buzzing with activity. I had some inquiry calls I planned to return and a call from Abe Whitmore – that was a biggie. After our brief conversation at the party the other night, I wasn't sure if he was serious or if he was just being nice. He owned a huge racing barn between Lexington and Louisville that stood several stakes winners and two Preakness winners. He wanted a farm spread done and wanted me to head it up.

I quickly jotted his number down and called his secretary to set up the appointment. Holy cow, we were on a roll. I checked on all the new projects, pleased with what the staff was accomplishing. We had quite a few interviews to do and some new clients, so I appointed some senior staffers to handle those and sent junior staffers and interns along to observe and learn. I knew everyone liked to get out of the office occasionally. I learned early that delegating responsibility was the most efficient way to get things done, and letting your staff take responsibility encouraged them to rise to the occasion. A few clients however, I intended to handle myself, starting with Nancy.

I stopped by the house for a quick lunch, leftover salad with peppery parmesan dressing from our favorite local eatery, Dizzy's Grill, just up the street. I changed into some clean capris with a white tank and peach tee, grabbed my laptop and the portfolio I had put together for the project and headed over to Excalibur Farm to work on Nancy's ad campaign for her stallion. I'd already researched his winnings and lifetime achievements and printed a list of all his get winning in the ring, but I needed to interview Nancy for the spread.

As I turned in the drive and passed through the stone gates, I took in the lush pastures and tall oaks lining the drive. I checked my GPS again, making sure I had the right address. This place did not look like a public boarding facility, though I couldn't recall what Nancy had told me about the farm, if anything. Immaculate black fences surrounded manicured pastures and a few horses grazed, tails occasionally flicking. The road curved and finally I saw buildings in the distance. There were four huge barns and more shed row barns to the side. A small brass sign with an arrow indicated BOARDERS. Holy Moly, this place was fancy. Another smaller road, marked with another brass sign reading PRIVATE DRIVE, wound around behind the barns. I could just make out the upper story and roofline of a graceful Kentucky mansion surrounded by a grove of centuries old trees. Excalibur Farm was indeed impressive. I followed the BOARDERS sign to a paved parking lot and pulled in next to Nancy's car, unmistakable because her license plate was WRLD CH6, for her stallion's six world champion titles.

I wandered up the aisle taking in the rows of pristine stalls. The horses were all munching on noontime hay. Some lazily looked up, ears flicking to see who was walking thru the barn. I had missed the smell of fresh shavings, barns and horses. An office/lounge was situated next to a large tack room. A note on the door read COACHES, TRAINERS and BOARDERS ONLY. I supposed this kept tourists out. Could tourists find this place? But I knew it wasn't uncommon for visitors to the area to avail themselves of any driveway, hoping to see some famous horses.

Not finding Nancy in the barn, I followed the sound of voices to the end of the aisle. To the left of the doorway was a large jumping arena. I peered around the corner, not wanting to interrupt. Nancy was cantering a large thoroughbred around the course, obviously finishing up a lesson. She took two final jumps and pulled up next to her instructor, whose back was to me. I started out the door, raised my hands to clap for Nancy's performance, and stopped dead in my tracks. *It couldn't be.* Although he wore a ball cap, those broad shoulders, narrow waist and that ass, hugged by well-worn jeans, could belong to no one else. A knot formed in my stomach.

"Good work today, Nancy." There was no mistaking that voice and I ducked behind the barn door, hoping he hadn't seen me. I took a deep breath and gathered my thoughts. *Oh sweet Jesus, I'm gonna have to face this guy.* My wanton behavior and later humiliation came rushing back to me. I briefly thought about sneaking out and calling later to reschedule, preferably somewhere I wouldn't have to see him. *No. He was the prick here, not me.* I took a step out again, determined not to show any sign of embarrassment. His back was still turned, and unbidden, mental images flickered of those thighs pressed against mine, his breath hot on my skin, his hands on my... *Stop it right now!*

"Mel! Girl get over here! Did you see me? Second lesson ever and this handsome young fella says I'm a natural." She patted him on the arm like a son and my eyes were drawn to his muscular forearms. I fought down the blush that was threatening to expose my discomfort. I had no choice but to approach the arena. I leaned against the fence, resting my arms on the top rail.

"Nancy! You looked great. So does this mean George has lost your heart?" I teased her, while studiously ignoring Jake. I knew that horse was the love of her life.

"Never!" she laughed. "But this is exhilarating! My goodness, I'm out of breath. This old lady is going to have to get in shape. I haven't been in the saddle seriously since I retired George. Whew!"

Jake turned and I caught my breath. Even through his sunglasses, I felt his dark eyes searing through me. His light grey t-shirt clung to his ripped body in all the right places and showed off his strong tan arms. His lips lifted in a little smile, his eyebrows rose quizzically and I knew he recognized me. *Oh kill me now.*

Nancy led her horse to the gate and Jake walked around to get it for her. He was so close I could reach out and touch him. His eyes locked on mine but he didn't say a word. We silently turned toward the barn. As the three of us neared the barn, a groom appeared and took the horse.

"Oh where are my manners?" Nancy stopped and faced us. "Mel, I'd like you to meet Jake. Jake Hamilton, meet Melanie Wainright. Melanie and I go way back to when she was just a kid. You two should talk. You have a lot in common." She was obviously oblivious to any tension in the air.

He stuck out his hand as if we hadn't met and I had no choice but to take it. Little sparks flew up my fingers and spread throughout my body like I'd touched a livewire. He looked pleased with himself. *"Asshole. You did that on purpose,"* I mentally shot at him.

"Wainright? As in Wainright Performance Horses? Melanie Wainright, multiple National Champion?" he asked. *Duh, asshole. So now you're impressed.*

"Yup," I answered, more curtly than I'd meant. "The same."

"Not my breed or specialty, of course, but even I know the name. Ya'll raised some nice horses if I recall - Arabians, Saddlebreds and National Show horses?"

"They bred my George, aka WPH Commander's Last Salute," Nancy chimed in.

A shadow passed over his face and his expression was more serious. "I was sorry to hear…" He didn't finish his sentence and I was glad he didn't. I got so tired having to tell people it was all okay when it wasn't. Life went on, of course, after the accident. But the event itself was never okay. They meant well, but they didn't get it. I got the sense, though, that maybe Jake did get it. I was curious as to why. *Don't get sucked in.*

I was thankful he hadn't asked about the farm or the horses, though he had to have known. If he knew about the accident, he also knew the farm and horses had all been sold as per my parents' will and the money put in trust for me in case things didn't work out in New York. The accident and subsequent sale had been big news in most of the major equestrian magazines, social media and blogs. At least I had the house. Jake might be a man-whore, but at least he was a sensitive one. The thought amused me. Amy would like that.

"Same time next week?" Nancy asked.

"Absolutely," Jake replied, smiling and revealing perfect pearly white teeth. "Maybe I'll get you converted from saddle seat horses." This charming, teasing side of him was new and a little bit of me softened towards him. No wonder all those women flocked to him. But not all the charm and good looks could make up for the fact that he was a player. I wasn't interested.

Nancy smiled indulgently and shook her head at him. She took my arm and led me to the client lounge. I felt his eyes follow us.

Nancy grabbed a water from the fridge.

"Water? Tea?"

"A water would be nice, thanks. This place is incredible."

"It is, isn't it? There's the main board barn, which also has this lounge and the locker rooms and main office. The other barns are training horses and sale stock. There are a few trainers that lease space in them, so there's always a ton of clients – makes things fun."

As she got the water, I took a seat on a comfortable sofa. The lounge was lovely. It wasn't just a typical client locker room. It was spacious, with soft leather sofas, occasional chairs and various tables. A dining table and chairs sat next to a small kitchenette. The floors were polished oak with rugs too expensive to be in a barn. The walls were adorned with framed photographs of all kinds of horses and riders. It might have been the most lavish client lounge I'd ever seen. My parents' barn, where we'd all kept our horses years ago, was nice, but this was in a different category altogether. It was fancier than my first apartment in New York. I set up my laptop on the coffee table. Nancy placed a bowl of trail mix on the table and took a seat next to me.

I pulled out my recorder and interviewed her for the article and spread. We talked business and discussed her goals and wishes regarding her horse and I offered up options how to proceed. She had no budgetary constraints, which made things much easier.

"I'd love to do some sort of reception," She added. "Something small, I think. Cocktails, maybe? Any excuse for a party, right?"

I laughed with her but she had a good idea and I was eager to work on it.

"I'll get something written up for you as soon as possible. And I'll get a draft for you to approve before we publish. I can also show you different layouts and schemes for the ads. As to a reception, we need to get permission to do it here I would think, since it's where your horse is. Think we'll be allowed?"

"Oh I think it can be arranged. Jake owns the place. I can talk to him. Or you can. You're both attractive young people." She chuckled to herself. "Don't deny it. You know he's a dish."

Well fuck my life. Of course Jake owned it. If she only knew what I'd done. Like this wasn't going to be completely awkward. I wanted to groan and pull my hair out. But Nancy was my client as well as my friend, and I couldn't let my transgressions interfere with business. Shit.

She refreshed our drinks and sat back down, pushing our work papers out of the way.

"Now. That's better, right? I swear I am so woefully out of shape. As much as I hate to admit it, age is catching up."

"Nancy, you've heard 'you're only as old as you feel' - or was that 'act'?" I laughed. "Oh well, either way, you're the youngest sixty year old I've ever met. Honestly, you're an inspiration."

She laughed out loud and slapped her knees. "Oh child, if only the body could keep up!"

I had to laugh with her.

"That jumping stuff? Like flying. Seriously adrenalin rush stuff - like the fanciest fire breathing, slobber slinging, big-trotting horses – they just get your blood pumping. I just didn't realize how technical it all was. I thought you just jumped things. Then I found out you have to count strides and stuff. I'm so glad Jake is a patient teacher. He's really such a wonderful person too. His students adore him."

Yeah, I've seen that firsthand. I thought of Miss Bouncing Boobed Blond from the party.

"What possessed you to try jumping of all things?" I asked.

"When I moved out here, this was the nicest boarding facility I could find. I just watched everyone and decided I should try it. And everyone raved about Jake as a coach. You know his students usually make the zone finals every year. Rumor has it, he was at the top of the list in the selection trials for the U.S. Equestrian Team when he was younger, but something happened and he dropped out. No one seems to know why and I would never ask. If I were younger, I'd totally go after him. But he's private. I've never seen him with a girl out here. He's never been married. I don't even think he's been engaged."

Just talking about Jake made my pulse quicken. The more I heard, the more intrigued I was. But I knew he was dangerous. He would only break my heart. I would not let that happen.

"Speaking of men…" I crossed my arms and made a funny face at her. "What's up with you and Abe? I have an appointment with him later this week so thanks for introducing us, by the way."

"You're welcome. And nothing. We're friends. We tease about dating but it isn't serious. We are far too independent and set in our ways." I thought I caught a wistful look on her face, but decided not to press the issue too much.

"If you say so…" I said, with a look meant to tell her I didn't quite believe her.

"Listen, hon, I need to say this," she said seriously, "and I know you probably don't want to talk about it. But your parents were good friends of mine and I feel awful for not reaching out to you when they died. I'm not good with that sort of thing. You know I've always thought of you and Amy as the daughters I never had. I hope you'll forgive me and I do hope you know that if you ever need anything, you can call me."

"Nancy, I know that. And you know we all loved you too. I'm so glad we've reconnected. And don't worry about it. It was really rough. Still is some days. But there was nothing you could have done. I hated people looking at me with pity and not knowing what to say. I felt almost as awkward as they did."

Nancy hopped up suddenly, pulling me with her. "Topic change!" she announced. "C'mon and say hi to George. Horses lighten any mood and it's getting a little heavy in here!"

That was Nancy. She had a unique ability to will herself and everyone around her to shift moods like a lightning bolt. She did not tolerate melancholy. She was firmly convinced that a positive attitude created a positive result.

We fed some treats to her beloved stallion. It was apparent that even in retirement, he was an amazing animal. His coat shone and I could see his muscles ripple under fine skin. I admired his powerful hip and laid back shoulder, which created the incredible motion that made him a world champion six times over.

"He's still incredible." I told her. And I meant it.

Nancy glanced at her phone. "Oh hell. I've monopolized your entire afternoon! I better let you go so you can do something brilliant!"

She hugged me tight. "Outside of our project, let's do lunch or something just for fun. Maybe you'll even tell me you found a hot man!" She exaggerated a sigh and I laughed.

Stepping outside, I paused, letting my eyes adjust to the

bright daylight. Across the lot, Jake was standing in the shade of a large oak, arms crossed, one foot resting on the rough bark, as if waiting for me. *Why?* I felt his piercing eyes on me, though I couldn't read his expression through his sunglasses.

I nodded slightly, acknowledging his presence. Obviously I'd seen him and I wasn't going to be rude. One part of me desperately wanted to talk to him - to get to know the enigmatic man who made my blood race. My heart pounded uncontrollably as I walked the across the shaded lot to my car. Out of the corner of my eye, I saw him shift suddenly, as if making up his mind. He strode over to my car and blocked my door before I had a chance to escape. *Whoa.*

He looked at me and took a breath, like he was struggling with what he wanted to say.

"I want..." he started but I cut him off.

"Did you enjoy the party?" I asked innocently.

His expression changed slightly as if I'd thrown him off-course. Maybe I shouldn't have been so flippant. But then his eyes narrowed and he brought his face closer to mine.

"Yes, actually…more than I expected." His sizzling gaze made my breath hitch and I swallowed hard. *Wow – that's uncomfortable. But two can play that game.*

"Pretty date you had. You get her home OK?" I shot back at him.

He seemed amused. "She wasn't my date, if you must know. But yes, she arrived safely home."

"Not your girlfriend?" I hoped I didn't sound too interested, but maybe I'd been wrong. My heart gave a tiny jump. I wanted to be wrong.

"Hardly." He smiled broadly and rolled his eyes. "Ex-client with too much money, too little talent and too much time on her hands."

I didn't realize I was holding my breath. I let it out slowly. He was still smiling. I caught myself staring at his lips and thinking about the blistering heat they created. When he lifted the corners of his mouth, his eyes crinkled and I saw the man so many people adored.

"You should do that more often," I murmured, looking down at my feet, slightly embarrassed. Why was I acting so juvenile around this man? Why did all my training, education and self-confidence fly out the window in his presence?

He took my chin between his thumb and forefinger and lifted my face to his.

"I should do what more often?" he asked.

"Smile," I answered simply.

He stood there looking at me, not saying a word. I started to feel self-conscious.

"So," I squirmed inside. "I better go, um, work or something."

"Have dinner with me," he said. It wasn't a question.

"What?" He completely threw me with that one. My mind raced. *I can't, I shouldn't. I don't want to get involved. I want him.*

"Have dinner with me," he repeated.

I just nodded stupidly.

"Good. I'll pick you up at 7:00." He stood looking down at me a minute longer. "You're so fucking beautiful, damn it."

He slid sideways and opened my door. I drove away quickly wondering what the hell just happened.

4

Judging by the laughter coming through the screen door, the entire neighborhood was in our pool. The wine bottles and margarita glasses told me all I needed to know. I popped my head out the door.

"Hi kids! I'm home," I said.

Sara, Steve, Amy and a few of our neighbors raised their glasses.

"Get changed and join us," said Amy

I check the time on my phone. "Can't. I have dinner plans, but I'll sit and watch you guys."

"Client meeting?" Amy asked.

"Ummm, actually no. I'm having dinner with Jake Hamilton," I told them.

Exaggerated gasps came from the pool. Really? Was it that surprising?

"You have a date with Jake Hamilton? Holy cow – what the heck did you do to score that?" Sara asked. I wasn't sure whether to be insulted or not. What did she mean by that?

"Do you finally have a crush on someone? This is too good!" Amy said.

"God! Lay off you guys! It's dinner, not marriage. I'm

allowed to go to dinner."

"Oh yeah right. What happened to 'I don't want a man' or 'I'm never dating again'?" Amy chided. "Wait – that guy from the other night – the hot one – that was Jake Hamilton? I've never met him, but I've heard…"

Sara interjected, "What? You're in business and you don't know Jake Hamilton? He's so dreamy."

Steve punched her playfully in the arm. "I take issue with that!" he laughed.

Amy glared at her and made a face. "Only by reputation, sorry to say. Maybe I'll get a chance to change that now, though."

"Ugh. You witches! I never said I was never dating. I said I didn't need a man. I alone am in charge of my own life. And I'm not dating him. It's just a dinner…so take that, Amy!" I huffed, pretending to be mad at her.

"I call bullshit!" Amy shouted. "You were flirting with him at the party. Oh and don't think I didn't see him checking you out. In fact, I think I pointed it out to you. So …"

I flipped her off and poured myself a Merlot.

"I saw that! Whatev, Mel. You like him. You're blushing."

"UGH! Impossible friends. I don't know why I hang with you people. See?" I pointed to my glass. "I need wine to deal! And as to your question, Sara, what do you mean 'how did I score that'? I was meeting with a client, and it just happened. So hard to believe someone would ask me out? And Amy – What reputation?"

"Hey Mel," Steve yelled from across the pool. "Don't let these gals get to ya! They're just jealous. Well, except for Sara. She couldn't possibly look at another guy with this fine hunk of man floating here." He looked at Sara and flexed his muscles. "But really, he's a super nice guy. We do work at the farm from time to time, you know. All his students adore him from what I can tell and he has a waiting list a mile long for lessons. But he's never been married, no kids – never even lived with anyone. He's seen in public with all these hot women, but none seem to last. And the big house? You saw it while you were there, right?"

I nodded, definitely interested.

"Story is, he won't set foot in it. Lives in the old caretaker's cottage out back. The stable hands think it's haunted. Only person ever goes in there is his aunt."

"Didn't she raise him?" Sara asked. "I heard his parents were killed when he was a kid or some such."

I felt something melt in me. I knew what that was like. I was grown when it happened, but still the pain was crippling at times. It had to have been ten times worse as a kid. I was more curious than ever about this man. Knots formed in my stomach. I was nervous as hell about tonight.

I got up to leave. "Guys, I better go get ready. Have fun talking about me when I'm not here."

"We want full details when you get back. And don't forget to pack condoms!" Amy said.

"Really, Amy. Really?"

"Hey Mel," Amy walked in as I was drying my hair. She was still in her swimsuit.

"Amy, you're dripping on my floor," I pointed out.

"Whoops!" she laughed and grabbed a towel. "I just wanted you to know, I really am happy for you. And I'm here to help you get ready, cause that's what best friends do."

"Amy, ya'll are making such a big deal of this, you'd think I was a hermit. Truth is, he didn't really give me a way to say no," I laughed. "And I'm pretty sure you're in no condition to help me do anything. However, I will admit to being a teeny bit nervous and so I will let you judge the final product. You really have to go put some dry clothes on and quit dripping on the floor. You don't want me to fall. Pretty sure a bruise on the head is not the look I'm going for."

"Whatever you say, Bestie. I'll be back in a jiffy." She gave me a sloppy damp hug and tripped off down the hall.

I laughed to myself. I pulled out a simple sleeveless summer dress. Short, but not too short. I had no idea what the plan was, but the dress with simple nude leather sandals should be appropriate for most anything. I fluffed my hair, ran my fingers through my bangs and stepped back to inspect.

My phone dinged on the bed. A text appeared in my inbox.

Unknown: Are you ready?

Jake must have gotten my number from Nancy. I sure didn't remember giving it to him. Shit. I didn't even give him our address.

Me: Just about. This is Jake, right?
Unknown: Expecting someone else?
Me: Not tonight.
Unknown: I'm ignoring that. I will be at your door in 10. At stoplight.
Me: Don't text and drive. Do you need address?
Unknown: Nope. Google Maps. Got it.

I saved his number to my address book.

"Wow." Amy came in and sat on my bed. "You look amazing. And without my help. Humph."

"Thanks. I think I'm jittery. He's almost here."

"Oh have a good time. It's been awhile. And I sure hope you aren't wearing panties under that dress."

I threw a pillow at her. "Amy, out!"

She ducked and ran. "Love ya girlie. Let me know when you get in. I'll be here all by myself!"

5

The doorbell rang and I had to fight the nerves down. What did he expect from this date? Was he really a love'm and leave'm kind of guy? That was kind of my M.O. Then again, I'd never felt an attraction this strong, and it scared me. I thought of his lips, his hands, his jeans with those thighs and that ass. *Stop!* I had to get control of this situation. This date was going to be on my terms. I didn't know Jake, really, and though everyone seemed to like him, I wasn't ready to be at his mercy. Truth be told, I didn't trust myself around him.

I opened the door. His dark eyes swept over me appreciatively and my throat went dry, butterflies jumping in my stomach. I couldn't speak.

"Hi," he said simply. "Ready?"

I nodded and slipped out before the rowdy crew out back could yell inappropriate things through the open French doors. We walked down the sidewalk until we reached the street.

"Hey, I have to apologize in advance. My car's in the shop and my farm truck is my only backup." He shrugged his shoulders sheepishly.

"More than ok. Makes you seem more – human - I

mean…" *What did I mean?*

He laughed easily. "Good. What? I assure you, I'm completely human, despite what you might hear. Remember, I told you I'm not a vampire – despite their popularity right now. Honestly I don't understand the infatuation you women have with that."

"Can't explain it myself." I found my voice as I started to relax. "I'm actually glad you're a real man. Otherwise, I'd be delusional."

"Oh, I'm definitely a man." Oh, yes. He was. He looked positively edible in his untucked button down polo and khaki shorts, his tennis shoes a reminder of his rebellious streak.

"Listen, I - I was thinking maybe we could walk down to our favorite restaurant. It's just a few blocks and it's a nice night," I said.

He smiled, "So…no trucks for city girl?"

"No. I mean, no that's not it." *Ugh. I sound like an idiot.*

"Don't trust me?"

I looked up at him. "Maybe." *And I know I don't trust me.*

"Then your favorite restaurant sounds fine."

We walked the few blocks to Dizzy's making some small talk about the weather. He brought up the party and how well attended it was and how much he'd heard they raised for charity. As we reached the front door, I turned to him seriously. I needed to get something straight and try to set some ground rules, which given the butterflies in my stomach and the sparks that flew when he accidently brushed against me, was more for my benefit than his.

"Speaking of the other night," I spluttered, "I want you to know I don't usually..."

He studied me seriously and shook his head slightly. "Yeah – about that – neither do I."

"Good. Now that we've got that settled." I smiled and let out an exaggerated sigh and shrugged my shoulders.

He opened the door for me. "Glad you made an exception. Glad I did too," he whispered in my ear. *Holy shit.*

We chose a table outside on the patio. The night was humid but not uncomfortable. Though busy, the restaurant was not so loud that we couldn't talk. Our waiter, with whom my crowd was well acquainted, appeared right away with menus.

"I know. A glass of Merlot and a water, Mel. And for you sir?"

Jake ordered a Merlot as well. He studied the menu. "So I take it you live here?" He leaned back, casually crossing one muscled leg over the other. The memory of those thighs parting mine sent shivers up my spine and my heart did a flip-flop.

"Not quite," I laughed, "but we're here often enough we probably should. Actually, the food's good, the wine's good and we can walk, which, if you knew my friends, you'd understand that's a good thing."

"If they're anything like Nancy…," he laughed easily. She's something else. *You've* known her a while." It was more a statement than a question.

"Been checking up on me?"

"When something interests me, I use my resources." His eyes met mine, and though he smiled, I felt the heat burn right through me. My stomach dropped a little and my thighs tingled. *C'mon, Mel, get your game on.* Usually I could control entire dates, but this guy was way ahead of me.

"So I'm a thing, now? Thanks," I teased.

He looked amused. "Some*one*, then. My apologies for word choice. You're much more than a thing." He touched my wrist with his fingers and slowly ran them up my arm. Goosebumps trailed behind his fingers. "You didn't answer my question."

Deep breath. Act natural. "Nancy was a combination of friend and parent to me when I was young. She used to take us on adventures our parents probably wouldn't have approved of," I laughed. "What, exactly, did you learn?"

"I'll leave you to wonder. Suffice to say, she's kept up with you."

I couldn't tell if he was teasing or serious. What did he know about me? *Damn it, Nancy.* I had a feeling he knew more than I wanted him too. He was way ahead of me. And I knew next to nothing about him. *Clever boy.* Thing was, a part of me wanted him to know me, and that scared me.

Our waiter appeared to take our orders, giving me a welcome chance to regroup. I ordered the salmon and Jake had a pasta dish. I took the liberty of another glass of wine. Its soothing warmth crept through me, and I grew bolder.

"So…" I asked, "stupid question maybe, but have you always ridden?" I wanted him to open up. I wanted to know a bit more about his man who took my breath away.

"Yeah, well. Depends on what you mean by 'always'. The farm's been in my family for generations, but I wasn't really interested til I was a teenager. Before that, I didn't want much to do with it. Living there, I just kinda took it all for granted, I guess. I didn't understand the obsession – never dreamed I'd make it a career."

"When something's readily available, you don't appreciate it as much," I said. *Was I talking humans or horses?*

His eyebrows rose sharply. He'd caught the unintentional double entendre. "I've heard that said. I think it depends on the situation." He met my eyes and held me captive.

Our food arrived, breaking the spell again, thankfully. But I no longer cared whether I was winning this game. I didn't even care about the game. Jake Hamilton was fascinating.

"Anyway, I started with the nastiest mare in the barn when I was 13. She was awful, just awful. Bucked, kicked, bit – ran off – you name it," he laughed. I could see his body visibly relax as he talked about the subject he was most passionate about. "I've no idea why I didn't just quit then. I mean she was enough to make showing chickens seem appealing."

"Ha!" I almost snorted. "Seriously? And you didn't give up?"

"Nope – she pissed me off. And she made me a better rider, though she never really got better. She was always a bitch, but she made me think like a horse. You had to work around her quirks to get anything done. Instead of getting mad, I had to learn to out-think her – not sure I really succeeded but hey – I was just a kid. Later I got a better horse."

I smiled thinking of my own parents who started me with a pony in the back yard – never dreaming one day we'd own a farm, breed national champion horses and travel the world with trainers and coaches. Our lives were simply consumed, and we had loved it.

"Well, I don't run in your circles, but I gather you've been rather successful. You seem to be the go-to guy with people lined up to get in your barn or just snag a lesson here and there. And you selected for the U.S. Equestrian Team? I may as well admit I googled you."

His eyes darkened and I saw a fleeting glance of something – what was it? I'd hit a nerve somehow. Subject closed. End of discussion.

Then his mood shifted and he grinned. "You googled me? I don't even wanna know. Oh hell – yeah – I do."

"You've never googled yourself? There's surprisingly little about you - no social media links - nothing but the odd mention here and there of clinic dates and some glowing reviews. How you've been this successful with hardly anything to show on the net is interesting."

"Well – I don't do social media at all. The rest? I don't know. Just lucky I guess. What about you? You were quite successful yourself. Ever want to return to it?"

"Oh, maybe someday. I need to concentrate on my career, so I don't really have time to devote to riding, nor the money. And I don't know if I'm ready after… Well, I don't want people to treat me differently, you know." I had no idea why I told him that. I probably said too much. I wanted him to tell me about his parents. After all, he obviously knew about mine. Googling him had revealed nothing but the fact that they'd been tragically killed. The lack of detail was surprising, given the amount of information readily available these days. What kind of mystery was hidden there? Perhaps Kentucky protected its own. My parents' story, by contrast, had been splashed all over the news, and not just in equine circles.

"What do you miss most? I mean about the horses," he asked.

I knew what he was doing, turning the conversation to a happy place, and I appreciated it.

"When you're on a great trotting horse, whether it's a Saddlebred, Arabian, or National Show Horse, there's just nothing like it. The crowds cheering, the music pounding, your heart pumping, the lights, the total adrenalin rush from knowing all that power is contained between your legs…"

"So you like power between your legs," he smirked.

"You're bad."

"I'd like to be worse."

Holy shit. He took my breath away. His dark eyes fixed on mine and his suggestive turn of phrase had my head spinning.

My phone dinged. I had a message.

Amy: Is he eating out of your hand yet, or do you need rescuing?

Me: Fine. Later.

Amy: Oh *Really*!!!!!

Jake asked, "Something important?"

"Sorry, I know that's rude. Just my roommate, Amy. She's checking on me."

"Perhaps I should walk you home before she comes in person to make sure you're okay," he laughed. *No. No. No.*

I'm not ready yet.

"Ha! No – she's just nosy, really. But I do have to work tomorrow, so maybe."

He insisted on paying, though I offered to split. Normally, I'd have insisted so as not to feel obligated. Amy told me I was weird for that. I didn't care. I liked to feel independent. But Jake was different. I knew I was giving up a bit of control, but I rather liked it.

We walked along the sidewalk quietly for a minute. The sky was unusually clear and the stars shone brighter than normal.

Jake raised his arm and pointed. "Big Dipper. See, just there."

I looked in the direction he was pointing. "And the Little Dipper there," I answered.

"You know your constellations?" he asked.

"Not many. My mom did though. We used to watch for meteor showers."

"My mom liked the stars too," he said quietly.

On my doorstep, he faced me. Though he barely touched me all evening, the charge in the air was palpable. He ran his fingertips down my cheek and tipped my face to meet his. His lips brushed mine. My pulse quickened and a fire ignited somewhere deep inside me. My response to him was immediate. Like a magnet, I was drawn to him, unable to stop the tumultuous riot of sensation that threatened to overpower me. I let go and lost myself in his kiss, my hands moving to his hair to pull him closer, our tongues tasting the depths of each other. He pulled back, gently pulling my lower lip with his teeth as he ended the kiss, leaving my knees weak.

He smiled as if he knew what effect he had on me.

"Thank you, Melanie. Until next time." And then he turned and walked to his truck, never looking back.

I stood inside, leaning against the door, trying to regain composure. *What the fuck?*

Amy, of course, wanted to know everything.

"Not much to tell. I mean, we went to dinner. We talked. We walked. And then he kissed me and left. That's it. And nothing more. I mean - he insinuated a lot, but he didn't try anything. Not one thing. Maybe I've lost my touch!" I laughed.

"Or maybe he just has your number," Amy said. "Maybe he's smart enough to keep you guessing. Maybe you've just met your match. I mean, he's not groveling yet," she laughed. "Heck, most guys disgust me, just watching them around you. I may even be a teensy bit jealous."

"Really? No. You're much prettier than I am. I just learned to flirt better – you know the whole batting eyelashes thing – gets them every time." I exaggerated a flirty wink. "But seriously," I sighed, "Amy, I swear. I don't know what to make of this guy. I just haven't let anyone in since – oh - never maybe. Even with the ex, I never let him know me fully, and that's probably what enabled me to wake up and see him for what he was and walk away."

"Stop. That guy was a con artist to a 'T'. You couldn't have seen it coming. He had us all fooled. But not all guys are like that. I'm still hoping for mine, but maybe you finally found someone who interests you, someone you can't control, tease and dump. Maybe he's got his own shit going on. Maybe he likes you for you. Fuck, I don't know. I'm happy you actually let yourself like someone."

"Maybe. There just seems to be more to him than the typical shallow guys. I don't know…there's something about him. He's intense but funny, very private and yet sensitive. I feel like I don't know everything – and for the first time in a long time, maybe I want to."

"Shit Mel, that's heavy," she teased, "but seriously, good for you."

When I went to sleep, dream man appeared. But this

time, he had Jake's face.

6

The next few days were a whirlwind of activity. I tried to tuck Jake into a corner of my mind and concentrate on work. I hadn't heard from him, which irked me somewhat, but I didn't allow myself to dwell. The staff of *Kentucky Equine* had produced an amazing amount of material and I was impressed by the quality of the work. The editors were swamped with copious amounts of copy and layouts. Clients had jumped on the new special advertising spreads, making the upcoming issue bigger and better than ever.

The articles were fresh and informative and our photographers and layout specialists had outdone themselves. Our once clueless owners had availed themselves of every opportunity to learn about every aspect of the magazine and they were learning quickly. They were also thrilled that for the first time in months, the magazine stood to earn a profit. I had dubbed this next issue our "re-launch" and the staff was determined to make it spectacular.

I emailed Nancy a copy of our interview and spread for her approval. I was pleased with the way it shaped up, but it was more important for the clients to be happy. And because she was my friend, I knew she'd be completely honest. I especially wanted her opinion before I met with Abe. I had really liked him when I met him, but his account would be huge and I couldn't afford to screw it up.

My phone dinged a message.

Nancy: Got your email. LOVE IT!
Me: Suggestions?
Nancy: None. Perfect.
Me: Glad you like.
Nancy: Haven't seen Jake. Did you ask about a reception?

Well, she obviously knew I'd been out with him, then. She hadn't approached him because she hadn't seen him, but she knew I had. Hmmmm. Still, I wondered why she didn't just ask him herself. She boarded there after all. Oh well, fine. I'd do it.

Me: Not yet. Will get on it.
Nancy: He's a good guy, Mel.
Me: what are you up to?
Nancy: Innocent of all charges. Working on upcoming horse show. Lunch sometime?
Me: Don't trust you but K.

Oh hell. She's doing it on purpose, making me ask. What was she up to? I smiled at the thought of Nancy playing matchmaker. If I hadn't been on a date with him, or that other bit from the party, I'd just call him like any other business call. But this was a little tricky. I was actually nervous about contacting him first. *Ugh. Suck it up girl.* I sent him a text.

Me: I need to ask you a question
Jake: Yes, I will take you to dinner tonight.
Me: Not the question

Jake: Then ask me tonight.
Me: ????
Jake: 7 ish
Me: Cocky much?
Jake: Hope so.
Me: OMG. You're bad.
Jake: Lesson here. See you later.

Amy wasn't home yet when I got there. I had a few hours, so I read the paper by the pool and then did some research on Abe. I wanted to be completely prepared for that meeting. If he was going to be a major account then I couldn't afford to fuck it up. My mind drifted to Jake. I hadn't heard from him since our last date and all of a sudden I was going out with him again. Not that I expected him to call, but I usually I was trying to lose guys. This one didn't call and then expected me to be available? Well, maybe he didn't expect. And what had Nancy been telling him? I didn't know what to think. This guy was playing my game. And he was playing it better than me. It was working. I was definitely intrigued.

After a shower, I chose a simple mint colored sleeveless sheath dress, short but not too short, that showed off my legs. I left my hair down and straight, sweeping my long bangs to one side. A pair of simple summer sandals and I was as ready as I was going to be.

"Wow! You look fab! Going somewhere special?"

I jumped at least a foot in the air, heart pounding.

"Fuck! Amy! How did I not hear you come in? My god, you scared the shit out of me!"

Amy laughed. "I think you were under a hair dryer when I got home. You should have seen yourself. That's what I call a YouTube moment!" At that point, she was doubled over.

"Bitch, I will so get you back! But yeah – I'm going out with Jake."

"Twice in a week. Is that a record for you? Something

going on? Do I need to stage an intervention?"

"Ha Ha very funny."

"Fine. At least this time, wear lacy panties."

"Amy! Oh – at least you're not suggesting I go commando," I laughed.

"Not this time. I figure you might need a barrier at this point!"

She laughed and darted out of my room.

I heard voices in the living room and stepped out to find Jake and Amy laughing about something. Jake took my breath away. Dressed in a casual polo and jeans, he was leaning on the bar. He turned to look at me and his eyes swept over me appreciatively, making me blush. He walked over and took my hands, sending shivers up my arms, my body instantly reacting to his touch. *How did he do that?*

"What's so funny out here? Sorry, didn't even hear the door," I said.

"I didn't even have a chance to knock." Jake looked amused.

"Well, I figured I needed to meet hunky Jake, here," Amy said, "Make sure he's OK for my best friend and all." I shot her a warning glance, which she ignored.

"And the verdict?" Jake asked.

"Jury's still out, but I approve so far." Amy pretended to check him head to toe. Jake laughed at Amy's antics and I relaxed a little.

"OK, you two. Have fun. Try to think of me here by myself with nothing but trashy TV." She waved us toward the door.

"I'm sure I won't remember you at all," I laughed, "and no texting me!"

7

"I'm still in the truck. I hope that's OK." We stood at the curb in front of the house. I was painfully aware of Jake's body next to me.

"I'm a farm girl at heart, despite my city stint. Trucks are cool."

He opened my door for me and put his hand on my elbow to help me up in the large dually. His touch set off a thousand sparks all over my body. What was it about this man?

He climbed in the other side and maneuvered the big truck out of our driveway. The truck was cluttered with bags of vet wrap, an odd leg wrap, some halters, a pair of boots, work gloves, assorted tools and a few needles and syringes.

"Wow," I said. "Where's the kitchen sink?"

"I told you it's a farm truck. I didn't know I'd still be driving it or I'd have cleaned it up a little."

"It's fine…it's just if you get stopped, they're gonna think you're a drug addict." I pointed to the syringes and bottles.

"Probably," He said. "I told you I don't take it out much. Not really date material, huh?"

"Listen…" I tentatively put my hand on his arm, trying to ignore the tingles that contact sent down my spine. "You don't have to apologize to me. I'm easy – shit - I mean…" I felt the flush rise up my neck until my cheeks burned.

His eyebrows rose. "Really? Do tell."

I made a face at him. "Asshole."

"And she has a potty mouth too, folks." He smiled and winked.

"No seriously, I'm just saying I'm not one of your models or heiresses or whatever that can't handle a little clutter. The fact I can live with my roommate should be testament to that! She's completely cluttered." I was yammering too much.

"OK, I get it," he chuckled. "And my models and heiresses, really? What other things have you heard about me?"

"Not much," I lied. "Just that you have a string of women hanging on your every word." I smiled to let him know I was teasing and not a bit jealous or curious. That was a lie too.

"I date occasionally. I'm a guy. But 'hanging on my every word'? I don't know whether that sounds like heaven or boring as hell."

I laughed. I liked this playful side of him.

"You're definitely not boring," he added.

"In a good or bad way? Or too soon to tell?"

"Definitely good."

We pulled up to a small Asian restaurant.

"I know it doesn't look like much, but I swear it's the best in town. They have the absolute best egg rolls. I hope you like Asian?"

"If I didn't you'd be screwed. But you're in luck. I love Asian food."

The hostess settled us in a booth near a window, handed us menus and took our drink orders. We both had tea. Jake refused to drink and drive and I didn't want to be the only one drinking. As much as I thought a glass of wine might help my sudden attack of nerves, Jake was intoxicating enough, and I wanted all my wits about me.

"Pretty much everything is good here. If you don't mind, I'll get egg rolls for appetizers and maybe an order of Shrimp Rangoon. You have to try it. And I think I'll have the Teriyaki Combo. Know what you want?" Jake asked. *Yeah, you. What was wrong with me?*

I nodded, "Sounds good. I think I'm going with the Cantonese Shrimp."

A waitress appeared and took our orders. She smiled oddly at Jake. "A lady friend this time Mr. Jake, yes?"

He smiled and nodded. "Yes, Mrs. Whong, a lady friend. Mrs. Whong, this is Melanie."

"Good," the older woman said. "Nice to meet you, Ms. Melanie." She took our orders and smiled at us again. "Good to see you, Mr. Jake." She took our menus. "About time," she muttered as she walked away.

I chuckled. "I take it you come here a lot."

"Can you tell?

"So Mr. Jake – do you never bring girls here? I think I'm flattered."

"Nope – guess I never have. But I told you, I don't date really." So what, he just had casual flings with beautiful brainless bimbos? What did that make me? *Play it cool, girl.*

"Oh – you just attack girls in fields?" I couldn't help myself.

"I hardly think I attacked you." I felt my face flush as he looked pointedly at me. "I'm pretty sure you felt the attraction too."

"Whoa. Ok. You win. I'm officially embarrassed. Time for topic change please!"

He grinned crookedly. "What if I don't want to? I distinctly remember every moment…and I'm hoping for more." His eyes grew dark with intent and I squirmed in my seat. I wanted nothing more than to pull him right over the table and feel his lips on mine.

How could this man be charming and flirtatious yet dark and dangerous at the same time? I had to admit, I was completely intrigued. He said all the right things, yet gave away nothing. Usually, I never accepted dates at all. Second dates were unheard of. And most men bored me to tears by the time we arrived at a destination. But this guy? I couldn't figure him out. And that was a problem for me.

Mrs. Whong brought our food and refilled our drinks.

"Wow. You were right. The food is excellent," I said between bites. "I see why you eat here so often."

"I'm here every other day or so. I guess that makes me predictable."

"I would never describe you as predictable," I said, looking up at him.

He grinned wickedly. "Now that I like."

We drove around downtown Lexington, looking at the city lights and watching the college kids roaming the local nightspots in the university district. Our easy banter over dinner had calmed my nerves and I stole a glance at him. His handsome chiseled face, framed by that thick dark hair, showed the effects of a life outdoors. The slight imperfections served only to highlight his extreme masculinity. He was no soft boy. He was lean, hard and all male. I wanted to touch him. *Ugh. What is wrong with me?* I could not let myself fall for this guy. But a little bit of me already had.

He took a strong hand off the wheel to change the radio station.

"Like this one?" he asked.

"*Royals*? Yeah. Good one."

"Good," he said and his hand strayed to mine. The touch caused my heart skip a beat and my breath came quick. He took my hand and entwined his fingers with mine. At first his touch was gentle, tentative, as if seeking permission. He increased the pressure, possessively claiming my hand while stroking each of my fingers with each of his, skin on skin, kneading, brushing, caressing. My heart beat erratically and I felt a slow burn building. I hadn't held hands with a guy since high school, but Jake made it an erotic art form. He was making love to me through our hands and I was completely turned on. His thumb caressed my palm and I stifled a moan.

I couldn't speak. I could only feel. Did he know what he was doing to me? I felt a yearning between my thighs that threatened to consume me. He never looked at me; just kept up that wicked assault on my hand and senses. His hand, fingers still interlaced with mine, strayed to my bare knee, his thumb brushing against my flesh, sending tremors up my legs. His hand inched higher to the edges of my skirt. I was throbbing and wet with anticipation.

He slowly untangled our hands and let his fingers explore under my skirt around the edge of my panties, reaching toward my aching core. His fingers eased under the flimsy lace, exploring the outer edges of my now slick folds. He slowly teased my tender swollen sex, creating a maelstrom of sensation.

"Anything you want to do?" he asked quietly. "Or anywhere you want to go?"

"Huh-uh." *To bed. With you. Just make this moment last forever.*

"Good. I'm taking you home." He pulled his hand back and broke all contact like a hot rock, both hands firmly back on the wheel of the truck his mouth set in a hard line.

What? What had I done? What happened? One minute I was about to come from the touch of his fingers, and the next he was dropping me off like he couldn't wait to get away from me. That's *my* game. I did that to men all the time. I never saw it coming. *Damn it.*

But we weren't headed to my house. Instead, we wound around a two lane back road covered with a canopy of trees so thick the moon barely peeked between them.

Jake didn't say a word. What happened to the easy banter of earlier? I didn't know whether to be terrified or turned on. Maybe a little of both.

"Where are we going?" I finally gathered the courage to ask. I knew my voice sounded small and I hated that.

"My house." Just like that – he didn't ask, just took it for granted.

Holy shit – not what I was expecting. But why did he seem so edgy? I didn't understand. He was obviously angry about something. And I didn't want to go to his house to fight about imaginary things. I'd done that with my ex.

"I don't…" I started but I couldn't find the words to tell him. *Tell him what, exactly?*

He just looked at me. "Tonight, I get to call the shots OK? I don't feel like sharing with prying eyes. I don't want speculation from others. I'm in uncharted waters here…"

What was he trying to tell me? Was this vulnerable Jake? I was confused, clouded - and I wanted him with every fiber of my being. But I had to be honest.

"Jake. You're scaring me," I said simply.

"I'm sorry," he said quickly. He took a deep breath, closed his eyes and exhaled. "I just - I don't bring people here...ever." He looked at me so seriously it frightened me.

Ever? He'd never brought a date to his house? My heart surged. I wanted to wrap myself around him, give myself to him and show him that I would never betray or hurt him. I wanted to open myself to him and let him take me to places I never dreamed of. *My god. What was I doing?*

He drove through the gates of the farm I'd been to earlier in the day. I wondered what the inside of that historic mansion looked like with its elegant southern columns and balconies overlooking the fields. But he kept following the road past it and drove around behind to a small cottage. So Steve had been right. Jake didn't live in the big house.

The cottage was white, like the main house, and mimicked the historic architecture – minus the sweeping balconies. Simple columns supported the wide porch. A couple of rocking chairs waited, shifting with the night breezes. Jake parked next to a picket fence and walked around to let me out.

He saw me glance at the big house.

"Yeah – I don't need much space. That shadow passed over his face again – but was quickly replaced by a wide grin as a huge dog came barreling toward us.

"Easy Snowball!" He scratched her head. "Meet Melanie. Melanie – this is Snowball."

Snowball was a giant of a dog. She shoved her large wet nose under my hand, asking for attention. I scratched her thick hair and she rewarded me with a slurpy lick.

"Wow! She's easily the biggest dog I've ever seen!"

"She's just a pup. She'll get bigger," he laughed, as my eyes grew round.

"Seriously?"

"Yeah. Great Pyrenees. They're great guard dogs - people, varmints and such."

She was licking both of us now, bounding back and forth and wagging her whole body. We stopped on the porch. Jake reached into a cabinet and pulled out a dog bone.

"Yeah I can tell – she's vicious." I laughed.

"Well, she does a great warning bark and, let's face it; she's so big not many people would stick around to see if she's friendly."

Playing with Snowball melted the tension in his face and body. Somehow, seeing him with this big dog, who obviously adored him, made my heart do tiny flip-flops. Yes, I was falling for him whether I wanted to or not.

He petted her as he pulled out his keys.

"Ladies first," he said as he ushered me in the door.

The door opened to a cozy living room with crown molding and wide plank wood floors, dark with age. A leather sofa, coffee table and a couple of eclectic antique chairs were place around an antique rug. A huge armoire housed a TV and an antique writing desk was in a corner piled high with papers and a laptop computer.

"Excuse the mess," he said quietly. "I didn't plan for company." He seemed almost shy. Another side of Jake Hamilton?

"It's lovely," I told him – and I meant it.

"Well, you can thank my aunt for that. This was her…well…our house when I was young. When I moved back here, after college, she redecorated it for me. I like it - she knows me well."

I wanted to ask about her but given his reaction to certain topics pertaining to his past, I wasn't sure I should. I tried to coax him out of his shell. I wandered about the room, stopping to admire some fine paintings of famous horses.

"She raised you, right?" I asked.

He looked surprised. Had I overstepped that hidden boundary already? But surely it was no secret. I did have friends here, he was a local celebrity of sorts, and heck – I'd admitted to googling him.

"Yes," he answered, "since I was ten."

"Does she live here on the property?" I wanted to steer him around to the big house mystery without overstepping.

"No. She has an apartment in town. Said she wanted something smaller and closer to the grocery. But she helps take care of things."

I stop near a photo of a beautiful young woman in a field, her dress fluttering in the breeze, a wide brimmed sun hat shading her eyes.

"Your aunt?" I asked.

"Mom," he said. That guarded look appeared again but was quickly gone. "Can I get you a drink? I'm afraid I don't have much – just milk, juice, water or beer."

"I'll have milk please," I said. The look on his face was

worth it. He cut his eyes at me and raised an eyebrow.

"OK – I'm kidding. A beer would be good, thanks."

He laughed, shaking his head and stepped through a door to what I assumed was the kitchen.

Obviously there would be no more discussion about the stunning woman in the photo. I looked around for a picture of his dad. I didn't see one.

He came back with two cans and handed me one. He picked up a remote and music softy filled the room. I pointed to another picture on a shelf of a small boy on a pony. The picture was obviously taken at a show and the boy was holding a blue ribbon and smiling broadly. There was no mistaking Jake.

"First blue?"

"Actually, yes."

"Adorable." I moved to the next set of pictures. A teenaged Jake smiled from atop a big warmblood. Tucked in the frame was an envelope with the official U.S.E.T. seal. I turned to Jake. I didn't know much about all that, but I knew it was special to have been picked and at such a young age.

"So you didn't go…." I prompted.

He was silent a minute, then answered, "Things came up." Another off-limits topic. What was up with this guy? Taking the hint, I checked out the other pictures from various shows.

He moved to stand behind me and began gently massaging my shoulders. His fingers ignited a firestorm of sensation throughout my body. I leaned my head back on his hard chest and his mouth blazed a trail down my neck, his hands roaming to the swell of my breasts. His fingertips created a string of shivers everywhere they moved.

"Cold?" he whispered.

"Hardly," I said. I wanted him more than I'd wanted any man. Ever. He pressed against me and his mouth tasted my shoulders, generating explosions of need. I felt his excitement through the soft denim of his jeans and I backed into him, rubbing against him. He groaned into my hair and turned me to face him.

"Look at me" he said.

I met his eyes and saw raw need that echoed my own. His lips crashed down on mine taking my mouth possessively. He bit my lower lip and his tongue darted in and swirled against mine. My arms snaked around his neck and my hands knotted in his hair. I returned his kiss eagerly, my mouth reveling in the taste and feel of him. I was on fire, blood boiling in my veins, a feverish craving building between my thighs.

"I want to know how wet you are for me," he moaned into my mouth. One hand worked in circles down to the small of my back, pulling me closer, pressing my burning apex against his demanding hard-on, which was straining against its confinement. His other hand strayed to my legs, his fingers grazing up my thighs, leaving tingling sensations behind. He slipped a finger in the edge of my panties and I gasped, the intensity of my hunger making my head swim. His fingers, working under the thin lace, dipped into my slickness and circled my clit. I melted against him. He brought his fingers to his lips.

"So sweet. God you taste so good."

I was incapable of speech as he guided me backwards to seat me on the sofa, parting my legs and kneeling to dip his head under the short skirt of my dress. His tongue caressed my thighs and I squirmed against him, unable to control my body, needing him closer. He pushed aside my panties and brought his mouth to my throbbing clit, sucking the sensitive bud while his fingers parted my slick folds.

"So wet, so ready for me," he groaned, the slight stubble on his chin creating more friction than I thought I could bear. His fingers slipped inside me, parting me, touching, exploring, and rendering me senseless as he stroked my inner recesses. My fingers dug in to his thick dark hair and he continued his delicious assault on my body.

"I want to feel you come around my hand."

His husky voice uttering such wickedly delicious words brought me over the edge and I gripped his shoulders, digging my nails into his skin, crying out as the warmth flooded over me, my walls clenching down on his hand as I came. I was panting, unable to catch my breath. He stood up, took a condom from his pocket, and placed it on the table before removing first his shirt then his jeans and briefs, freeing himself. His engorged cock was heavily veined with desire and I leaned forward, emboldened by lust, and guided him into my mouth. I cupped and kneaded his balls while my tongue danced on his cock, making him tremble. The power was exhilarating and I felt a craving building again from the depths of my being.

"Jesus, Mel. Slow down, I'm not gonna make it," he said, his voice strained.

I smiled to show him that was exactly what I wanted.

"No. I want to be in you. I want to feel you come on my cock. I want to pulsate deep inside you and make you forget anything and everything before me."

He lifted my head and kissed my nose, my cheeks, and my chin.

"This has gotta go," he said as he lifted my dress over my head and tossed it to the side. He brought his lips to my breasts, teasing the rounded flesh above my bra. He slipped his fingers underneath and teased my nipples until I cried out. He expertly unhooked the straps and let it fall, his tongue and teeth and hands biting and sucking and pulling until I squirmed and pulled him on top of me.

"These too," he said, pulling my soaking panties down and tossing them. He looked down at me, dark eyes devouring me in a searing glance. He grabbed the packet from the table, ripped the foil with his teeth and slid on a condom. He lowered himself and I felt his hardness at my entrance. I raised my hips to meet his, needing him -

needing release. He entered me slowly, letting my flesh adjust to the width of him before sinking into me, filling and stretching and causing ripples of sensation as my body took him in. I wrapped my legs around him, pulling him deeper. He slowly moved within me; thrusting, circling, thrusting again, teasing me into a frenzy of balled up heat. He slipped out slowly, leaving me aching for him to fill that void. He rubbed my swollen clit with his thumb, and then, grabbing my hips, he thrust into me hard, taking his pleasure, the full length of him buried deep in my folds, touching places I didn't know I had.

"Jake," I cried, my breath ragged.

He stilled.

"You OK?"

"Don't stop. Oh please don't stop. Not now."

His eyes darkened with desire and he plunged into me again, thrusting over and over. My hips kept wicked time with his; the strain on his face showed how close he was to the edge.

"Take me Jake. Come with me."

That was his final undoing. He drove into me, and my body bucked with the force of my orgasm, aftershocks wracking my body and mind. His body tensed, his cock rigid and he threw back his head as his body shuddered, his cock pulsating, spilling his release.

We lay, a tangled mess of arms and legs, panting and sweating, drained of the ability to move or think. He lifted his head from my chest and gently took my lips with his, brushing a stray hair from my eyes with his hand.

"Holy fuck, Mel. What have you done to me?"

"I'm sorry. Ask me again when I can move," I replied, smiling at him. I never knew sex could be that earth shattering. And beyond that - the connection I felt with Jake was something I'd never felt. I was that girl who reveled in her independence - the girl who needed no man.

Somehow, that night, I knew that had changed. But I also knew Jake had secrets; something he was holding back that I couldn't put a finger on.

I suddenly felt very tender and I stroked his soft hair, slipping my fingers through its silky strands, drinking in the scent of him – of us. *Jesus, don't lose it, Mel. Don't get hurt.*

He rolled off the condom and wrapped it in some tissue.

"I hate those fucking things," he said.

"Better safe than sorry, though," I answered. "I'm glad you're safe. Or…was I a forgone conclusion?"

He looked sharply at me.

"No. You were certainly not a forgone conclusion. I admit I wanted you but I really didn't plan this…and here."

He looked troubled.

"I'm glad you brought me here," I said quietly. "Have you been…?"

"Tested?" he finished my question for me. "Yes, of course. And it's been a while since…"

He didn't finish his sentence but I knew what he meant and a secret part of me was relieved he hadn't been with anyone recently. And apparently he'd never brought anyone to his house – his private sanctum. Why did he want to keep people as far away as he could, resisting attachment? And why did he break his own rule with me?

"Me too," I told him, "on both counts."

"Are you…?" he started.

"On the pill?" I answered, "Yes. Seemed silly to stay on it, but I'm glad now that I did."

"Me too. Because I would love to be in you, feeling you with no barrier."

I felt a twinge of lust between my legs. *Already? Wow.* I raised my face from his chest to look at him.

"I wouldn't want to get you pregnant," he said. Then he added, "I told you - I don't do relationships."

Really? Was that necessary to say? I winced, not meaning

to. I hoped he didn't notice. Why did that hurt? We weren't even dating really. I had no one to blame but myself. That bit about never bringing women to his house? Was that just a line? It was a good one and I'd bought it, hook line and sinker. It might have been nice to know I was just a conquest. Not that I expected declarations of love on a second date, but the depth of deceit was reprehensible. I wasn't hurt. I was pissed. I'd confused my pent up sexual frustration with something more and let myself want it. Eh, what the fuck. He didn't owe me shit. We'd had a good time, thank you, and at least I'd finally had an orgasm with a man.

"Look, jeez, Mel. I didn't mean to hurt you."

I sat up and a sigh escaped before I could stop it. "It's fine, Jake. It's been a lovely evening really, and that was maybe the most mind blowing sex I've ever had, so thank you, I'm spoiled forever," I said trying to keep it light, "but you should probably take me home. I have all those projects to work on and tomorrow is a work day."

I sat up and started to collect my things. He just sat silently. I saw him watching, like he wasn't sure what to do, fighting some internal impulse. He reached out and grabbed my wrist as I was reaching for my shirt. I turned to face him and saw on his face a sadness and disappointment that broke my heart.

"Stay," he said simply.

"Why?" I asked.

"Because…because I want you to. Because I want to hold you tonight. Because I think you want to and because…" he didn't finish.

What the hell was wrong with me? I shouldn't want to stay. I shouldn't want him to want me to. If I were smart, I'd walk out of here right now. If I stayed, he would hurt me eventually. He had already admitted as much. But he was right. I did want to stay. And what if he was telling the truth? What if this was uncharted territory for him? What if? *No, No, No, Mel.*

"Jake, I'm sorry. I shouldn't be upset. I don't expect anything – I don't have a right to. I'm here freely of my own accord. I'm not saying I want to get married, for god's sake. I don't even know you that well." I blushed thinking of what we'd done. "But I don't fuck around, despite my behavior tonight. And if this was a one-night-stand, it might have been nice to know up front. And if that's all this is, then fine. I'm fine. My mistake. But I'm not spending the night. Does any of this make sense?" I was rambling and I knew it but I didn't care.

He let go of my wrist. "Mel, I'm not good at this. I do casual. I've never done relationships because I don't want to build expectations. But with you, things are…different. You are not a one-night-stand to me. I want more. I want to be the only man who sees what you look like when you come and I want to be the only man you dream of at night. In my experience, bad things come of relationships, marriage and kids, but that doesn't mean you mean nothing to me. I want you to stay. I - I need you to stay."

He pulled me into his arms and looked into my eyes. I saw the loneliness there and if I were honest, I knew what that felt like. My resolve melted. We were two people who didn't want to be alone but were terrified of giving in.

Jake led me down the hall and into his bedroom. He turned on a lamp by his queen sized century old tester bed. "If you need the bathroom, it's through that door," he said and pointed to a door on the left.

"Thanks," I murmured.

The light switch was an old-timey push button affair. I pushed the top one and an antique overhead light flickered on. An ancient claw foot tub took up one side and a pedestal sink sat beside it. I padded across the black and white tiled floor and checked myself in the mirror above the sink. *Ugh.* I quickly splashed water on my face and cleaned myself as best I could. I stared at myself again, wondering who that girl in the mirror was and what the hell she was thinking. I could still leave – and probably should. And yet, I couldn't. I didn't want to. No – I made my decision and I was sticking to it. I looked around feeling suddenly modest and grabbed a t-shirt from a shelf. It hung about mid-thigh and enveloped me deliciously with the smell of Jake. Self-conscious I reentered the bedroom. He had apparently gone back to the kitchen – two glasses of ice water were on the bedside tables.

"Thanks," I told him quietly.

"You're beautiful," he said, "and my t-shirt thinks so too."

I looked at him and stuck my tongue out. "All I could find," I said.

"Come here," he commanded and pulled back the coverlet. I climbed in the bed beside him. He was completely naked under the covers, a little lascivious grin on his face. My stomach quivered in anticipation.

"Really?" I asked. After what we just did, I didn't know any men that had the stamina for more.

"What can I say? You inspire me."

I felt his erection hard against my thighs. His hand traced a line down my side and I giggled as he hit a ticklish spot.

"Ticklish much?" Delighted with his discovery, he continued brushing his fingers along my sides til I was holding myself in a ball, laughing uncontrollably.

"Jake," I gasped, "Stop!" I giggled more.

"God you're sexy when you wriggle like that," he teased. Then he wrapped his arms around me, and rolled us over so that I was on top of him.

"My t-shirt's going to be sad," he said and pulled it over my head. He pulled me forward and took one of my nipples between his teeth, nipping lightly, while the other hand pinched and teased my other breast. Liquid fire ignited between my thighs and I felt myself moisten, readying myself for him. Letting go of one breast, he reached between my legs to stretch my folds with his fingers.

"God you're wet for me already. Minx."

He alternately rubbed my sensitive nub with his palm and gently squeezed the base, sending spasms up my spine, the conflicting sensations creating a pleasure too intense to take. I took his cock, heavily veined with readiness, in my hand, rubbing myself with its head. Jake groaned and I lowered myself onto him, savoring the feel of skin on skin, no barrier between us. My body relaxed to take all of him and I sank down further, pushing him to my core. He was so deep my sex clenched around him and I rocked into and against him, then swiveled my hips, creating sweet friction against my clit while his steel shaft worked my sensitive inner walls. I heard a moan escape my lips and I let my hands map his hard body, glistening with sweat. That delicious tortuous build began. He grabbed my ass and held me suspended while he thrust his hips up into me driving him deeper than I thought possible. I placed my hands on his chest and felt his rapid heartbeat as he shifted a little and his cock rubbed against that inner place that sent my mind reeling. My sex convulsed around him. I was teetering at the edge, unable to stop.

"Oh my god!" I yelled as I came violently, a shudder rocking my body, my head awash with sparks of bright color. He groaned loudly, his mouth clenched. He drove into me hard, sparing nothing, and erupted with a final thrust, his warmth spreading within me. I collapsed on top of him, his hands clasped in the small of my back. I felt his aftershocks and his cock trembled inside me before going still. We struggled to regulate our breathing.

"Amazing," he said. "You are amazing."

"No – you are," I told him. "I never knew…"

He got up and I gloried in the sight of his body - taut, toned and rugged. He left the room and returned with fresh ice for our waters and a towel, which he used to gently clean me and then himself. He tossed the towel to the side when he was done.

He kissed me tenderly, soothing my lips with his softened mouth. He wrapped his arms around me and I rested my head on his shoulder, one hand on his chest. He took my other hand in his, entwining our fingers. Thus connected, a heavy satisfied darkness enveloped me.

8

I awoke the next morning and languidly stretched, with an involuntary smile on my face when I thought of the night before. I rolled over and realized Jake wasn't there. The sun was streaming in the window – what time was it? *Damn!* I noticed a note propped on my glass on the nightstand.

Sorry – early lessons. You looked peaceful. Text when u get up.

I smiled and reached for my phone. I wrote him a text.

Me: Am up finally
Jake: Almost done. How do you feel?
Me: Fabulous, if a little sore.
Jake: Good.
Me: Good?
Jake: You can't forget me
Me: Highly unlikely
Jake: I can take you home in a bit or…
Me: I have to work!

Jake: sigh. Be there as soon as I can.

I picked up my things strewn about the living room and blushed, remembering all we had done and said. My dress was in sad shape and I decided if I had to do the 'walk of shame', I shouldn't do it in that dress. I dug through Jake's drawers and found a pair of cutoff sweats that weren't horribly too big for me. His t-shirt hid the fact that I had to roll them a few times. I put some toothpaste on my finger and swished it over my teeth.

My phone dinged with a new message. Shit. There were a dozen messages from Amy. My explanation was much too long to text. I just called her.

She picked up immediately. "Where the hell have you been? Are you OK? Did you do him?"

"Oh my god, Amy. It's okay. I'm at Jake's. And, maybe."

"What the fuck? OMG –you little slut!"

"Amy, jeez, really?"

"I stayed up last night and even stayed sober waiting on you. I wanted a total play by play! Oh hell – was he good?"

"Thanks for caring," I laughed wryly, "and none of your business."

"Yeah, whatever, bitch. You got it bad. This is just too good! You are not living this one down. And you *will* tell me everything."

"Amy, I'll be home soon."

"OK. But the sex…" she insisted.

"Mind blowing," I told her.

She squealed, "Oh I knew it! Oh boy, ugh, I think I'm jealous."

"Hey, Amy. Gotta run, I think I hear Jake. I'll see you this afternoon."

We hung up just as Jake came through the door. Damn he looked good. His hair, windswept from being outside, fell over one eye. He swept it back and kicked off his boots by the door. He smiled and it lit up his entire face.

"Morning, gorgeous," he said. He walked over and took me in his arms, lifting me off my feet and kissing me. He smelled of trees and leaves and morning sunshine. My heart gave a little leap.

"Morning to you too. Good lessons?"

"Not bad," he said, "but seeing you here in my t-shirt and sweats – now that's even better."

"OK, bad boy, you have to take me home. It's a weekday, for goodness' sake. I have appointments to keep. By the way, I want to run something by you."

"Uh-Oh. Sounds serious," he grinned. "Should I be worried?"

"I don't know? Depends. I was supposed to ask you about Nancy having a reception to promote her stallion. She wants to do it here – just something small… Anyway, how do you feel about it? Having it here at the farm, I mean."

He hesitated for a minute. "I don't normally…" he started, but then he shook his head. " No – you know what? It's fine. At the barns, right?"

"Yeah, that's where the horses are, silly."

"Then, OK. You girls cook something up. It's fine. I'll deal."

"Thanks Jake. We'll make sure to get your approval before we finalize anything. Nancy's going to be thrilled. Nothing she likes better than a party."

He laughed. I picked up my few belongings. "I really have to go, you know," I said.

"I know. But it'd be tempting to keep you. I'm going to be gone a lot this weekend coaching at a show at the Horse Park. I'll call or text you…if you let me."

"I'd like nothing better."

Fortunately, I had already planned to work from home

to prepare for my meeting with Abe. I called the office anyway, to make sure no one needed anything. Then I called Amy to let her know I was home.

"I know you want all the scoop, but it's going to have to wait. I have got to get ready for this meeting at Abe's."

"Seriously?" Amy said. "Abe Whitmore? Wow. I'd love to have his insurance account. His horses are worth a fortune – not to mention the farm."

"Well, maybe we can work on that," I laughed – but I really meant it. Amy had done me some huge favors and I owed her a few.

"Let's plan a girl's night. Pick up a movie on the way home and I'll pick up dinner on the way back from Abe's."

"And wine," Amy laughed. "You can't forget that! See ya later, roomie."

I quickly showered and put on a pair of khaki slacks and a white silk blouse, casual but businesslike at the same time. I pulled my hair back in a loose twist. I folded Jakes t-shirt and sweats and placed them on a chair near my bed. My mind drifted to yesterday. Back at my own house, last night hardly seemed real.

9

Abe's place was breathtaking – black fences, white barns, green pastures. The office was lined with photos of various stakes winners and the wall-to-wall trophy cases were filled with silver platters and cups, evidencing decades of winners bred by the farm. The original family all died off leaving only a few heirs that cared nothing for the horse life and, rumor had it, Abe came from nowhere and bought the place lock stock and barrel. Where his money came from, no one knew.

Some people adored him and some never really accepted him. The old guard, the Kentucky bluebloods, tried to snub him, but over the years his money and good nature prevailed and they begrudgingly allowed him admittance into the inner circles. Now in his sixties, having reestablished the farm as a premier breeding and racing facility, Abe still showed no signs of slowing down. He was just as ambitious as he had been when he arrived 20 years ago.

He was said to be gregarious and generous and he had a way with the ladies. He'd been married once, but it had ended when he'd dallied with an heiress half his age. Apparently he had an ongoing flirtation with Nancy, too, though she'd never allowed it to go anywhere.

"So, Ms. Wainright, I hear great things about your talent. Incidentally, not just from Nancy, if you're wondering. I only use the best – but my connections in New York had you as one of the top talents when you left." He smiled. He was polished, distinguished and possessed of impeccable manners. Behind his grand mahogany desk, dressed in expensive slacks, starched yellow shirt and navy blazer, he was in his element. It was clear he was a savvy player. He'd done his homework. I wanted his business.

He pulled out files and we spent an hour discussing the farm and what kind of write up he expected. He wanted to know if we'd be interested in doing press releases as well. I told him I was sure we could accommodate, if I had to do it on my own hours.

"Well – Ms. Wainright - Melanie – may I call you Melanie? I like you and I'm impressed with your ideas. I look forward to doing business with you. You know if I were a younger man…" He winked and laughed. Business concluded, we both relaxed, free to joke.

"Abe, now that we're on a first name basis, you should know I don't mix work and pleasure," I said, making a stern face.

At that, he threw back his head and laughed out loud. "Nancy said I would like you. Said you were sharp as a tack when you were just a little thing. I believe she wasn't wrong. Speaking of Nancy, put in a good word for me please. I think she takes me for an old rake. Rebuts me every chance she gets. I suppose I should give up, but our little game has gone on so long, I'd miss it. Maybe one of these days…" and he laughed again.

"You know, I thought I sensed something there. I'm not sure she thinks you're serious. If you don't mind my saying, I think you're both stubborn as mules and doubly pig-headed – though those animals might protest at the comparison." I raised my eyebrows and smiled to make the point. "Nancy's an inspiration to me. You know I found her taking a jumping lesson yesterday, if you can believe that."

"I do believe it. Damn fool woman is going to break her neck."

I could tell he was fond of her.

A tall sandy haired man appeared in the doorway. "Ah – here's my attorney. Tom, come on in." Abe waved him in and motioned him to take the chair beside me. "I signed those contracts you left. I'll get the rest of the paperwork ready and we can ship those mares as soon as I can get the health papers. By the way, Tom, this is Melanie Wainright. Melanie, Tom Dillon."

"Nice to meet you, Melanie." Tom had a good firm handshake and a brilliant smile that lit his whole face. He was drop dead gorgeous in that All-American athlete way. The cut of his expensive dark suit showed his muscular build. He was probably in his mid-30s and I noticed he didn't have a wedding band. His blue eyes sparkled with a zest for life. He was immediately likeable.

"Melanie here is with *Kentucky Equine*. She's going to be doing a feature on the farm, among other things. She's just arrived from New York."

"Really?" Tom asked. "I graduated from NYU, and thought about staying to practice in Manhattan. Many of my friends did – boy we used to have some fun there. But Kentucky is home, and there's nowhere I'd rather be."

"I'm going to take Melanie on a tour of the barns, Tom. Want to join?" Abe asked.

"I've got a little time before I have to be back, so I'll come for minute," Tom said, "but I'm dressed for court, not barns today – so no adjusting horses."

Abe laughed and explained, "Melanie, Tom's father is an equine chiropractor, and before law school, Tom actually studied and got his chiropractic license."

Tom nodded. "I'm still involved with horses, though. My specialty is equine law. Contracts, disputes, torts, insurance – you name it. If it involves the industry, I probably handle it. Still, Abe here thinks I should pull double duty." Tom winked at me conspiratorially. "Sometimes he's pretty persuasive."

We all laughed easily as Abe showed us around the impressive layout. Stallion row was a veritable who's who of stakes winners and the mares were equally impressive. Weanlings romped through the pastures and we stopped to watch before heading back to Abe's office.

A smaller, intense man stepped out of the office next door to Tom's. "I've got those earnings reports, sir."

"Good, good. I'll have a look in a minute. Derrell Smothers, this is Melanie Wainright. Derrell is our accountant and bookkeeper here. If I had to do everything, it would all be half-assed – and that is intolerable to me. Delegation is key, you know. However, my evening reading consists of financials, breeding records and racing statistics. I enjoy it with a little wine," he joked.

Derrell didn't smile. He was one of those serious numbers guys. He was nice looking in a studious kind of way. I wondered what it would take to make him truly laugh. He looked like he could use a laugh or two. I choked back a chuckle as I recalled Amy saying she didn't trust mathematicians; that they were too linear to appreciate good food, art, wine or sex. She would definitely say this guy needed wine and sex. Through the door in his office, I saw some pictures of him on a horse. Apparently, he used to show jumpers, though from the look of him, he hadn't ridden or seen the outdoors in a while. He reached out to shake my hand, his clasp surprisingly weak and damp for someone who used to ride. "Nice to meet you," he said, pleasantly enough. He smiled, his eyes sweeping over me, holding my hand longer than necessary, the touch sending a crawling sensation up my spine. *Ugh*. I'd have to nip this one in the bud.

"Derrell pretty much revamped the entire system here," Abe explained. "Everything we do is on the computer now. So much better than the old ledgers. Of course, his job was a little easier than mine. When I bought this place, I didn't have the great team I do now. The books were a shambles when I first took over. It took a while to make sense of what the family had done. They let it go for years. And not just the finances – the breeding and foaling records were nothing but notations in spiral bound notebooks, if you can believe that. Derrell and Tom, here, keep us rolling right along now. But, that's why I only deal with the best. Now, with the touch of a finger, I can pull up any report and know exactly what's going on."

Derrell finally relaxed and smiled. Abe seemed to think a lot of him, so I figured I should give him a chance, though I still had reservations. There was just something I didn't quite trust.

"So, are you from here originally?" I asked him.

"Heck, we all were in school together," Tom interjected. "He and Jake Hamilton used to run together quite a bit." He turned to me, "I was the black sheep. I played basketball while these kids were hitting the show circuit trying to be Olympic stars."

I thought I saw Derrell's face darken briefly, but then he smiled. "California called. I bummed around out there for a while."

"Bummed around, my ass," Abe laughed. "While he was showing up the local riders out there, he graduated *Summa Cum Laude* from UCA and went on to become a CPA. Lucky for me, he came home." He glanced at his phone. "All right, folks, I have to return some calls. Say, Melanie, if you don't have plans tomorrow night you should come to the Galleries. I'm hosting a small cocktail party."

Derrell looked at me, "Don't let him kid you. He's donating a painting, an 18th century oil of King's Lass, a mare belonging to the Royal Stables. They are having a reception to unveil it."

"I told him he needed a tax write-off. He may have

gone overboard," laughed Tom.

"Wow," I said, genuinely impressed. "I'd love to see it."

"Good! Then come. It's informal - just cocktails and some finger foods. And Tom here has a date we're eager to meet," Abe teased. "Apparently my brilliant bachelor attorney met someone interesting the other night, though he won't tell us who."

I rolled my eyes. "You guys are ridiculous. But I'd love to come."

10

It was a lovely evening so Amy and I took our food and wine out to the pool. We hadn't been sitting long, when the back gates swung open and Steve and Sara appeared with more wine.

"Hey guys! Want company?" Steve was precariously carrying four bottles and two glasses.

"Looks like you could have used a bag." Amy twisted her mouth making fun of him. He made a wry face back at her and carefully set the items on the outdoor bar.

"Ha! I'm a real man. I got this," he said. We all laughed when one of the glasses tipped and he jumped to save it.

"Keep telling yourself that, Steve," I said. "At least you didn't stoop to boxed wine."

"Hey now. Some of that new stuff is pretty good! Steve's got a rare night off," said Sara, throwing their towels over a chair and plopping down in another one. Steve cannonballed into the pool next to us, sending a spray of water our direction.

"STEVE!" We all yelled at once, giggling.

"A rare night off, huh? Well why the hell are you two hanging with us then?" Amy asked. "Not that we aren't terribly fascinating, but..."

"Because you've got a pool and we have wine!" Steve said. "And it's cheaper than going out."

"True that." Amy raised her glass and we all toasted to cheap entertainment. "We were planning a quiet girls' night complete with pedicures and a movie, but hey, I am never one to turn down good wine."

Sara giggled, "Oh! We didn't mean to interrupt. You can always shoo us off. But frankly, I needed to get away from the house. I've been repainting our bedroom. Steve says it was fine the way it was, but I was just sick of the lime green walls. I've no idea what the former owners were thinking."

"Birth control," laughed Steve.

"Ugh, see? Hush up, you. Anyway, I have all this time until school starts, everyone's been gone all week, and I figured now was the perfect time to try my hand at painting. But, I have to say, I need a break."

"When you get done with your house…" Amy hinted.

"Not a chance in hell, girlfriend," laughed Sara.

"Steve – we haven't seen you around much. What terribly interesting cases have you had lately?" I asked him.

"Had to sew up a mare that ran through a fence today. It was particularly gruesome, but missed the artery so she'll be okay. Worked a couple of colics and saw a foal with tendon issues. But that's an easy day comparatively. Big deal is the virus."

"What virus?" I asked.

"You haven't heard? There's some new strain of infectious equine disease – mosquito born we thought, but at the rate it's spreading, may be contact or even airborne. Showed up in Texas, then Colorado, and now there's an outbreak in Ohio. They're getting really sick – and five have died so far. We've sent the bodies to the labs for testing but it'll be a while before we know anything. It's not here in Kentucky yet, but with show season in full swing, and so many animals being transported, it could spread fast. In the meantime, the state is considering quarantine – and other states are cracking down about imports and some aren't allowing horses across state lines without proof they don't have the disease – and we can't even really test for it yet. It'll be devastating to the state's economy if we can't get it under control."

"Shit," Amy said, looking grim. "I haven't had any calls yet – but I'm sure I will. If horses start getting sick or dying, we'll be filing all kinds of claims – mortality, loss of use, major medical." We were all quiet. If something as dire as an epidemic took place, all our livelihoods would be affected – the thought was sobering.

"The state vets' office hasn't released anything official. They don't want to start a panic until we know what we're dealing with. It's not a secret, obviously, but we don't want to scare people unnecessarily. Still, some sort of action by the state is probably imminent."

"Gotcha," Amy said, "Hey, thanks for the heads up."

I turned up the radio. "Guys – it's Friday night. Time for worrying tomorrow. Tonight let's eat, drink and swim!"

"Here! Here!" Sara opened another bottle of wine. "Hey – I found this one at the store the other day. It's really and truly called 50 Shades of Gray! Can you believe it's a wine now?"

Amy laughed, "It'll go well with the Ménage a Trois we just drank."

"My heart can't take it," laughed Steve.

"You mean your man-parts," poked Amy.

"I don't' read that mommie-porn romance shit," he protested, "Unless, of course, you girls are up for experimentation."

"Not on your life!" Sara giggled and punched him on the arm.

We all fell into gales of laughter.

I was a bit tipsy when I climbed into bed. I hadn't heard from Jake. It was only that morning that I'd seen him, and I knew he was coaching at a show, but still, after mind-blowing sex like that and our more serious conversations, I thought I might hear from him. I argued with myself. To text him or not to text him? My wine fogged brain won, and I sent him what I thought was an innocuous text.

Me: How's the show going?

Several minutes passed with no reply. Fuck it. I pulled up the sheets and turned out the light.

Ding. My phone lit up with a message. My heart flip-flopped.

Jake: Busy
Me: Doing?
Jake: Things.
Me: Things? Guess that's better than people?
Jake: I'd like to be doing one person.
Me: And that would be?
Jake: You.

I felt a rush of warmth in my nether regions. How did he have that effect on me? I tried texting him some more, but he'd obviously fallen asleep or gotten busy with something because there was no answer. I fell asleep dreaming of Jake and the things he did to me.

11

I'd been so busy; I hadn't given much thought to Amy's big date. She'd been so excited and I felt like a heel for not being a better friend and asking her for more information. I hadn't even asked his name, and if she'd told me, I'd forgotten. Epic fail in the friend department. After I got ready for Abe's party, I knocked on her door. She was putting the final touches on her make-up, and as usual, she was stunning.

"Amy. Wow. You look gorgeous."

She smiled, "Thanks, Mel. I have to admit, I'm having sweaty palm syndrome. Me! Of all people!"

"I've been a bad friend. Between work and Jake, I've been off in my own little world. I've laid my shit on you and haven't even let you tell me about yours! Forgive me?"

"Duh! Of course. Look, you never take any guy seriously, so I knew it was a big deal for you. I date quite a bit, so why would you wonder about this one? But I have to say, for some reason this guy feels different to me. I never, ever get nervous for dates. What's up with this? I've talked to him a couple times on the phone, and we've been texting. It's just too easy I guess - I don't know – maybe I don't trust it. We have actual conversations, you know? It isn't just flirting and sexual innuendo. So I'm nervous about tonight."

I laughed, "Maybe he likes your brains and not your body for once? Or he likes both? Or - maybe he's a eunuch and doesn't know how to tell you?"

"Oh. My. God. Stop. That's good, really good," she laughed. "Ugh, you are going to make my make-up run. But I'm proud of you. That's something like I would say!"

"I know. I learned from the best," I winked at her. "So where are you going?"

"We're going to dinner and then to a thing at the Galleries."

"Seriously? That's where I'm headed a little later. That's Abe's party."

"Yeah, Tom said it was hosted by one of his clients."

"Tom? Gorgeous Tom? Blue eyes, white teeth, athletic Tom? I can't believe I didn't know! I just met him yesterday at Abe's!"

"Well? Am I crazy? Not my usual type, huh?"

"I honestly really liked him. And he's hot. I approve wholeheartedly. What a small world. And apparently he grew up with Jake and this guy Derrell, who is Abe's accountant and office manager."

"Maybe I can pick his brain for you? Get the scoop? Really, though, there's something about him…" Amy said.

"Hey Amy?"

"Yeah?"

"Don't forget your condoms!"

The doorbell rang. I darted out of Amy's room before she could respond and greeted Tom while Amy was finishing up.

"Tom! What a surprise! Good to see you again. I didn't realize yesterday…"

"Good to see you too, Melanie. I didn't put two and two together either. So you're Amy's roommate. I may need advice from you later," he whispered with a wink.

"Glad to help any way I can," I told him.

I took a cab to the gallery. Being solo, I didn't want to chance driving if I had a drink. Abe met me with a warm hug at the door. He was busy greeting all the guests so I looked around and spotted Nancy across the room. She saw me and waved.

"So. You and Jake, huh. I knew it." She looked pleased with herself.

"Well – I don't know if we're a 'thing', but we did go out a couple of times this week."

"Hmmmm…and he *was* running a little late the other morning for my lesson. Looked a little sleepy. Would that have anything to do with…?"

"I have no idea what you talking about," I said innocently. Nancy was too much. "So Abe's looking mighty nice tonight. Maybe you should take your own advice and see what happens."

"Child, this old woman's too old for complications like Abe. I prefer to watch you youngsters – far more entertaining." But she glanced in his direction anyway, and I knew she was lying to herself.

"I think you should give him a chance. This flirtation's gone on long enough from what I hear. Anyway, I think he's really into you, more than you know."

"Why? Did he say something to you?"

"Maybe," I hinted, giving her a taste of her own medicine.

"Humph. Ok listen, on a different note, can you swing by the farm tomorrow? I want to show you something. Everyone's gone to a show and we can have some girl time with horses."

"OK– I have no plans. I'll come right after lunch. Sounds fun."

Amy and Tom came in and I joined them as we looked around the gallery. I'd never been, and it was impressive. Derrell saw us and walked over. Tom introduced Amy and explained that we were roommates.

"Two beautiful women in the same house. Tom, you

are a fortunate man," Derrell said.

Amy and I looked at each other and laughed politely. It was apparent he was a little awkward, but trying to be nice.

"Derrell, buddy, there's only one woman I'm interested in right now. No offense, Mel."

"None taken," I laughed.

"So you two went to school together?" Amy asked.

Derrell nodded, "Tom was the athlete. We didn't really run in the same circles, but yes. Of course, our parents were friends."

"Don't let him kid you. He just studied more than the rest of us. Derrell's parents' house was the place to be on weekends. Everyone who was anyone was there. And they had a barn that was the envy of Lexington. This guy," and he pointed to Derrell, "had his choice of mounts for any show. My dad was there all the time working on the horses. Of course, right after we graduated, he ran off to California without so much as a goodbye. Chasing girls and fun in the sun while I decided it was better to go to the wintry East to school. What was I thinking? But we're all here now. Derrell is the best damn CPA I know. Abe got lucky."

"That might be laying it on a little thick," Derrell laughed. "Abe pays better than any firm I ever worked at, and that's saying something. As for sunny California? Yeah…it was nice. But Tom, you know I had to get out of here." He paused for a minute and then explained. "My sister died that year. Our house was wrecked. My parents were in a bad way and I was just a kid and didn't know what to do. So I left. But," he said lightening the mood, "I got my shit together and now I'm back here."

"Oh wow," I said, "That must have been awful for all of you. I lost both my parents not too long ago, so I kinda understand."

"Hey, can I get you a drink?" he asked, turning to me.

"Sure, love one. Merlot?"

"Coming right up. And I'd love to show you around

the gallery. I overheard you say you'd never been."

"That sounds nice," I told him.

We strolled through the rooms, stopping to look at paintings, sculptures, and memorabilia from races and shows in a display dedicated to Kentucky's history with horses.

"This is pretty amazing," I commented.

"Yeah. They've managed to accumulate some nice items. Some they purchased and most were donations from generous benefactors. It's great for tourists to the Horse Park - the history of the horse in art and sculpture. Come – over here is Tom's painting."

We walked into another room, and gorgeous oil was highlighted in the center of one wall. I knew little to nothing about art, except to appreciate, but even I could tell it was a masterpiece.

"Holy cow. It's fantastic," I said.

More people were behind us waiting to see it up close so we stepped to the side. Derrell was proving to be a lovely host and friend. As I talked to him, he seemed less awkward. I figured he was just one of those hard to get to know people. Understandable. We all had our battle scars.

"So you've worked for Abe for a while?" I asked.

"Only about five years, more or less. I had sworn off coming back here, but he convinced me."

"But you have family and friends here. Tom and Jake."

He looked sharply at me. "I wouldn't call Jake a friend."

Wow. Ok. I must have looked surprised.

"Don't tell me you're taken by him too. Another Jake Hamilton groupie. So willing to be used and spit out."

"Ummm…hey. Sorry. Didn't mean to get into your personal history. I thought Tom mentioned you all were friends."

"Tom might be friends with him, but I know better. Look, just stay away from him, if you know what's good for you." He changed topics with a shake of his head.

"Sorry. Didn't mean to ruin a mood. Have you seen the bronzes outside?"

"Only from a distance," I answered. "Let me visit the powder room and then I'd like to see them."

What was up with Derrell and Jake? Did Derrell know something no one else did? Had something happened between them? Everyone seemed to adore Jake, but Derrell apparently knew another side. Jake was so private, it was hard to tell what could be true. I decided Derrell didn't need to know I'd been seeing Jake. Hell, I didn't even know what it was we were doing. Were we seeing each other? I thought of our night and felt a flush of warmth spread through me. I thought of his hands on my....*Damn it! Stop!* I really needed to control my train of thought.

I was washing my hands when a tall blond swished into the bathroom. *Oh hell.* She smirked at me, tossed her hair and entered a stall. I didn't think she recognized me. *Was that smirk her natural look?* Pam, that was her name. *Stupid drunk bimbo.* I left before I was forced to talk to her. I supposed that woman made the rounds of every social gathering. I knew the type.

I found Derrell and we walked out to the memorial garden to see the life-sized bronzes of famous horses. It was fascinating stuff. Nowhere in the world celebrated the horse like Kentucky.

We were heading back inside when I saw him. And her.

Pam was all over Jake like a dog on bacon. *Why was he even here?* I was stunned speechless and stopped dead in my tracks, heart pounding. He was supposed to be working. But there he was, with Pam positively drooling, her barely concealed cleavage all pressed against him. *Did she even have on a bra?* If he moved, I was fairly sure she'd fall over. He wasn't even pushing her away. *Fucking asshole!* I felt like a fool. Obviously, he didn't know was I was going to be there. I hadn't told him. But would it have mattered anyway? I didn't want him to see me and tried to steer

Derrell the other direction. I saw Abe and found my excuse.

"Hey, there's Abe. I haven't gotten to talk to him yet," I said and hurried away from Jake and the offensive Pam.

Abe was all smiles. "Turned out great, yes? I hope you're having a good time. Derrell, you showed her the museum? Good. Good."

"It's been absolutely lovely," I told him. "I've an awfully lot of work to do though, so I'm probably going to call it an early evening. Thanks so much for having me. Oh – and I talked to Nancy. I'll keep working on that for you."

He laughed, "Good to know I have a friend in my corner. She'll give in one of these years." His eyes twinkled. "Sorry you have to go so early. Did you see Jake? He was asking about you earlier. I told him you were here." He winked as if I ought to be swooning over Jake. *What, like everyone else?* Derrell had been right.

"I ummm, think he was busy or something. I'll catch him later," I said, hoping my voice wasn't shaking too much. I was furious, but I hoped I hid it well.

Abe looked confused for a minute but shook it off. "Well, OK then. Mel, we'll talk soon. Derrell, see you Monday."

"Can I give you a ride?" Derrell asked.

"Oh, no. You stay and enjoy the party. I'm just really tired. I can get a cab home. No problem."

"Well, I'll walk you out then," he said.

I turned and that's when I knew Jake saw me. *Damn it.* I hooked my arm through Derrell's, who looked surprised and unfortunately pleased. *Shit.* I did not want to lead him on. I liked him as a friend and only that.

"I need to tell Amy I'm going. Help me find her?" I should have extricated my arm from Derrell's, but Jake could not see me crumble. He needed to know I wasn't one of his willing admirers, to be cast aside at a whim. It was a childish, schoolgirl move on my part, but in that moment, I wasn't thinking straight. The night had gone to hell in a hand basket.

Amy and Tom were near the exit when we caught up to them. Amy's eyebrows rose when she saw my arm in Derrell's and I tried to signal with my eyes that we would discuss this later. I said my goodbyes, and Derrell walked me to meet the cab.

"Hey. Thanks for showing me around the museum, Derrell." I pulled my arm out from his and stepped back. "I really hope we're going to be good friends, especially seeing as how we're obviously going to be working together a bit." I tried to make my intentions, or lack thereof, clear.

He gave me a friendly hug. "I'm looking forward to it."

I turned my head to smile at him before getting in the cab. The next thing I knew, he'd pulled me close and his lips were on mine. I was so surprised; I did nothing for a few seconds before pushing him back a little. I lost my balance on the curb and almost tripped backwards, but Derrell reached out just in time and pulled me back, his arms around my waist.

"Oh! Uh - thanks," I said, meaning it. "But Derrell, what the…? I didn't …"

I tried to pull away but he didn't let go. Not wanting to cause a scene, I shimmied out of his embrace. He grabbed my arms and held on a little too roughly.

"Derrell! Stop it!" I hissed.

"Mel, I – forgive me. I…"

But he didn't get to finish his sentence before a hand pulled him back. Jake moved between us. "I think the lady said 'No'. Get your hands off her, Derrell," he threatened. His stance was relaxed but I noticed his hands were balled into fists at his sides.

"What? You think you can claim and destroy all women? You think you're that special? This is between Mel and me. You have no right to…"

"I'm serious." Jake's voice was deadly.

I couldn't believe what was unfolding in front of me.

Who did Jake think he was? He was with another girl, for god's sake, and I was perfectly capable of handling the situation without him.

"What the fuck people!" I was livid. "I don't belong to either one of you. I am not property. Jake, I can take care of myself, thank you. You can go back to your date. Derrell, I don't even know what to say. I can't deal with either one of you right now." I jumped in the cab and slammed the cab door. "Drive," I said.

I lay in the dark. My phone dinged an incoming text.

Jake: Mel, can we talk?

I stared at it for a minute and clicked it shut.

It dinged again a few minutes later.

Jake: Mel – seriously. I need to talk to you. I'm asking. Please.

What so he could screw me over again? No thanks. I'm done. I turned my phone completely off.

I was doing just fine on my own. I was doing just fine until *he* got under my skin. *Fuck.* I started crying, which made me feel weak, which pissed me off and made me cry harder. I pulled up the sheets, took a deep breath and closed my eyes, trying to shut out the whole night. Dream man didn't make an appearance, with or without Jake's face.

12

The sun was up when I heard our door. I called from the bedroom, "Amy, that you?"

She bounded into my room and bounced on the foot of the bed, landing on her knees. Her makeup was smeared and her red curls looked like they messed with the wrong brush, but she had a huge grin on her face.

"Good night, I take it?"

"Oh. The best. My god. Tom." She hugged herself. I laughed at her. "No, you don't understand," she said. "Mind-boggling. Oh, and did I mention he's nice too? I thought it was too good to be true – you know, a good guy and fantastic in bed? But yes, you can have it all." She stopped for a second and looked at me seriously. "Ok so Jake was there, yet you were arm in arm with Derrell. I just know there's a story there somewhere. Spill it."

I climbed out of bed and we made breakfast while I told her my version of the night's events.

"Holy shit!" she exclaimed. "I didn't see Pam, that whore. But Jake did ask me about you. Right when you left. That's why he went outside. Holy fuck, Mel. You do cause trouble."

"I just don't know. I didn't mean to lead Derrell on. I

was just trying to be friendly. But yeah, I also wanted Jake to know I didn't need him. Hush. I know. Behavior unbecoming and all that. And Pam. Ugh. I really thought Jake and I were onto something, you know? I mean, all that stuff about never taking anyone to his house and all?"

"Maybe he got scared," Amy offered.

"Well, I don't need that kind of scared," I said. "But I'm glad your night was successful."

Amy lifted her glass of milk in a mock toast "Your mess, my success!" she chirped.

"Oh Lord, Amy," I groaned, "You rhymed again!"

We fell into fits of laughter. I loved my best friend.

Thankfully, there were no other cars in the lot at Jake's barn. I scanned the area, but the coast seemed clear. I had promised Nancy I'd meet her. I was a little nervous about running into Jake, even though he wasn't supposed to be around. Then again, he wasn't supposed to be at the party last night either. Nancy was waiting inside for me.

"Come see! Come see!" she fairly dragged me down the aisle. She stopped in front of a stall. "Well? What do you think?"

In the stall was a huge, powerfully built bay horse that had to be at least part warmblood.

"Nancy, don't tell me. You bought a jumper."

"Well, I had to justify those lessons, you know."

"You are absolutely nuts and that's the most backward reasoning I ever heard. You know that, right?"

She laughed, delighted with herself. "I know. It was a crazy impulse, but I'm not getting any younger and you can't take it with you! Anyway, he's sweet as he can be and I adore him. But I've got something else to show you too."

She led me a couple of stalls down.

"Now this one you will like a lot, I think," she said.

"You got another new horse?"

"Not just any horse. This is Commander's Kharisma. I

call her 'Lissa' for short. She's one of George's first foals. You know I bred him a few times while I was still showing him. Figured it wouldn't hurt to have a few babies on the ground when I promoted him for real, and I wanted to see if it was even worth breeding him. She's out of an Arab mare, so she's double registered."

The young dark bay mare was gorgeous. She had a star and three white socks, good legs and good feet. She had a terrific neck that seemed to come straight up out of her shoulders, high set and hooky, with a well laid back shoulder, relatively short back, and powerful hip. Yes, she was a beauty.

"Lord, she oughtta be able to motor," I said. "She's damn near perfect. Is she under saddle?"

"For a year. The owners were aiming for the futurities, but couldn't take her. The wife got sick, the horses were put up for auction and I got her for a song. She's four so she has another year of junior horse. I'm thinking maturities this year if I had the right rider." She looked pointedly at me.

"Oh, no. Nancy, don't tempt me. I'm out of practice. I have a career and no time."

"And it's high time you came out of hiding and rejoined the show world. It's been damn long enough. Time to get back on your horse, dear. Anyway, how can you be in Kentucky and write about horses, if you're not participating?" She grinned slyly. She had a point – a skewed one - but still a point.

I sighed. "I'll think on it Nancy. Best I can do. But your offer is terribly intriguing, I admit." Actually, it was more than intriguing. I felt a long dormant sense of anticipation build inside me. It had been a long time since I'd seen a filly that nice, much less ridden one.

"Uh-huh. Whatever, Mel. You can say no all you want. But I recognize that light in your eyes. And look at it this way. I need to get her out there and seen. Eventually, I'll probably sell her, hopefully for a lot more than I have in her. So I really could use your help. And frankly, you need this too. Just think on it."

"I will Nance, I promise. She really is amazing. When she's settled in, I'd love to see her move."

"Shall we plan for one day later in the week? At least just ride her once."

"Fine. You got me. You know I want to ride her. I better do some exercises or something because I know I'll be sore as all get-out after!"

"It's settled. I'll call you on a quiet day and we can ride together. I miss that. Maybe I'll pull George out and let him strut his stuff."

We talked a little more and fortunately, she didn't bring up Jake. I wasn't sure she even knew what happened and I wasn't ready to discuss it, especially since I suspected she talked to Jake more than she let on. Eventually, I was going to have to confront the issue if I was going to be riding Nancy's filly at his place. I needed to quit worrying and put my big girl panties on. I had done nothing wrong. And men were assholes. I followed her into the lounge and perched on the edge of the desk as she stepped into the restroom to change.

"So your neighbor, Steve? The vet?" she called through the door.

"Yeah. Good guy. He and Sara come over quite a bit."

"Well, he was here the other day and was telling us about that virus going around. I hope it doesn't reach Kentucky. It'll be hard on the economy if that happens. I'm managing three horse shows over the next few months and I'll admit - I'm worried about them."

"Surely, it'll be OK. By then, they'll probably know exactly what it is and already have a vaccine. He did say they were working 24-7 on it. It's all over the country. They found a case in Michigan now too. They just don't know how it's spreading."

Nancy stepped out, back in her street clothes, and put her riding gear in her designer duffle.

"I hope you're right." She glanced at her watch. "Oh Lord. I'm going to be late. Mel, I've got to run."

"Something fun, I hope," I hinted.

"If you must know, I'm dining with our mutual friend Abe tonight. I'm not sure what I was thinking but somehow, last night, I think I agreed to go out with him. What was in that wine, anyway?"

"Ha! I love it! Wait til I tell Amy!"

"Laugh if you will. Somehow I knew you would derive some sadistic pleasure out of this."

"Not at all, Nancy. Ya'll are perfect for each other and you know it."

"I just hope he doesn't take Viagra," she said.

"T.M.I. Nancy. Really? Like I needed to hear that? But – uh - for your sake, I hope not either."

I hopped off the desk and gave her a quick hug before she left the lounge.

I stepped into the restroom to clean up before heading to the car. I washed my hands and stared at myself in the mirror, wiping a smudge of dirt off my cheek. I looked tired, but thankfully, my eyes weren't too puffy from crying the night before. I held my chin up and straightened my shoulders. Maybe riding again would be good. Riding had always been my therapy, my escape. Work and riding. No men. I knew I'd been right to swear off dating. I could have handled the one night stand. But for Jake to show up the very next night with that Pam thing and then go all possessive freakazoid? Too much. That was weird. And I'd lived in New York.

Head up, I walked out the door. And smack into Jake. *Fuck my life.* I hadn't even heard the trailer and cars pull in from the show. In an alternate universe, I would have made a smartass comment, but I wasn't in the mood. Apparently neither was he. We both stood there in silence, the tension mounting, my hands on his chest. My heart was pounding with a force I was sure echoed down the barn aisle. I could feel the rise and fall of his chest as his breath hitched. And then his lips were on mine and the voltage from the contact caused my heart to skip a beat.

I mentally resisted. I should have slapped the snot out of him. I was pissed for fuck's sake. But my traitorous body responded, the charge running up and down my spine, my mind numb, my lips parting for his insistent tongue. Without breaking the kiss, he backed me roughly against the wall, his mouth taking mine, claiming it, possessing it. His tongue flicking against mine starting an inferno between my thighs that I was helpless to stop.

He broke the kiss, eyes smoldering. "You. Are. Mine. I alone tempt you." And his lips took mine again with a crushing force. I took him in, savoring his hunger and I felt his cock hard against me. I struggled for air as his kiss overwhelmed me and gasped when his hand deftly unzipped my jeans and his fingers plunged into my burning depths. I shuddered as his palm rubbed against my clit, his fingers buried in me, stroking those places only he had reached. My hands found their way to his thick hair and I held on to his head as if for life support, our mouths locked together, tongues entwined. His other hand found my breasts under my shirt, pushing up my bra and teasing my nipples hard, first one then the other.

He moved us away from the wall and backed me against the desk, his hard thighs on either side of mine setting off a firestorm of need within me. Our heavy breaths, pants, moans and groans were the only sounds filling the room. He pulled his hands away to quickly dispose of my jeans and lifted me onto the desk. I held onto his strong arms for support as he unzipped his fly, releasing his engorged penis, beautiful in its fury. I gasped as he parted my legs and filled the void with a hard thrust, burying himself deep within me. My legs reflexively wrapped around him, holding him to me. My fingers dug into his back and slid down to grip his ass. The feel of his muscles contracting with each pounding thrust sent a thrill up my arms and fueled my undeniable scorching lust. I took all of him, my body opening, my blood on fire. I felt myself on the edge of that precipice, ready to fall over the edge as he plunged into me repeatedly, his cock hammering a rhythm my body sang to. Starting between my legs, my orgasm shot through me, my body shaking uncontrollably, muscles contracting in soul wrenching glory.

"*Fuck, Mel,*" Jake cried, his mouth buried in my neck, his body convulsing as his liquid heat surged into me, filling me and drenching my inner walls.

We didn't, couldn't move for moments. I collapsed against him, my arms around his neck, his arms around my waist, our breathing struggling to regulate, his penis still convulsing aftershocks within me. I didn't want the beauty of this moment to end. I felt tears threaten to spill over my cheeks. He overwhelmed me. I was obsessed and addicted and I hated him. I needed him with every fiber of my being and I didn't want to. I knew we had to talk…but not yet, just not yet.

He slowly backed away from me and helped me to my feet. He gathered my shirt and jeans and I was suddenly terribly self-conscious.

"Mel, I'm sorry. I…" he paused. "I had no right. Are you okay?"

I nodded and slipped my shirt on. "What are we doing Jake?"

"I don't know. I don't know." He ran his hands through his hair, messy from my fingers. "You have a right to see whomever you wish. I won't get in your way."

"What? Jake, what are you talking about? I'm not seeing anyone else. But obviously you are, so even if I was, I don't see that you can judge."

"But Derrell – you and he - all night…"

"He's just a friend. And yes, he tried to kiss me and I told him no. That's all. But I don't see that it was any of your business – and then you barged in. I mean, Pam wasn't enough for you?"

"Pam? Jesus, Mel. I told you. I'm not interested in her. She turns up everywhere I go and hounds me to death. I feel sorry for her. I don't want to be mean. She has problems. But I was not with her. I only went last night because I knew you were going to be there. I can't get you out of my mind. I can't concentrate for thinking about you. I can't sleep at night because - because I want you.

"You have every right to be mad at me. I don't know what I'm doing. I'm over my head. I told you I don't do relationships. I don't get that close. I don't let myself care. I don't get involved. But damn it, I can't leave you alone. I can't stand the thought of you with anyone else and I know if I don't step up, there's a million guys waiting to take my place and I can't live with that. Damn you, I care. Okay? Is that what you want?"

I didn't even know what to say. I don't know what I expected but not that. I knew it took every ounce of courage to spill his guts like that. And I knew it had only been a few days. I knew it was ridiculous. I knew I was falling in love with him. But he had secrets and issues and I didn't know how deep that went. He was so in control of his own world and so out of touch with anything personal. If I allowed myself to love him, I was giving him the power to hurt me. Could I risk it?

I looked him straight in the eyes. "I really hate you right now…" His eyes searched mine, worried. "…because you made me care. For the first time in a long time, I want more. And that scares me, because I don't know if you can give it to me."

His eyes softened, relieved. He nodded seriously. "I don't either. But I know I want to try - if you'll let me." He took his hand and gently wiped a tear from my cheek. I hadn't even known it was there.

Voices outside shook us from our spell.

"Oh Shit! Jake!" I hopped into the bathroom with one

leg in my jeans and one arm through my shirt. The jeans leg caught in the door and I opened it again, yanking the leg through as the lounge door opened and laughter filled the room. My heart raced and I tugged my clothes on, straightened my hair, wiped my red eyes and tried not to look as if I'd just had a mind-blowing orgasm on the desk the clients were now walking around. I flushed the toilet for good measure. Jake caught my eye as I stepped out, merriment evident in the devilish turn of his mouth. I raised my eyebrows at him and motioned him outside with a roll of my eyes.

His clients, flush with success from the weekend's show, were cracking open wine and beer and discussing the weekend. Jake waved away a proffered beer. "Ladies, it was a great weekend, but I'm exhausted so I'll leave you all to the celebrations and see you for lessons this week."

"Later, Jake. Thanks!" They looked at me curiously but I was in no frame of mind to be introduced. I'd face that crowd later.

Jake walked me to my car. "Call you later?" he asked.

"I'll be furious if you don't."

"I've always heard make-up sex is fun, but that was..." He closed his eyes and shook his head. "Yeah so anyway, maybe I like you furious."

"Jake!" I shook my head at him. "Go get the trailer unloaded and take a nap. Then call me later."

"Take a nap? I'd rather take you. But if you insist..."

I waved at him as I pulled out of the drive. I needed some time alone to think.

13

"Well? How do I look?" Amy had another date with Tom and was more excited than I'd ever seen her over a guy.

"Like a goddess, as usual, silly. Where are ya'll going?"

"It's a surprise. I've no idea. What are you up to tonight while I'm off with my hot guy?"

"Hanging right here in my trashy pink PJs, eating trashy nachos, watching trash TV and maybe getting a little work done."

"Oooooh! Trashy nachos night?" she giggled.

"Yup! And you are jealous."

"Actually, you know I love some trashy nachos almost as much as you like Hot Pockets with wine, but no. I think my plans win. But you know I'll be thinking of you every second I'm gone."

"Ha! No you won't, Bitch. And the Hot Pockets with wine was an adolescent phase. You know that."

"Right. Like you said. I know better. But you're right. I lied. I'm not planning to think of you at all!"

The doorbell rang and Amy grabbed her clutch and checked her makeup one more time in the hall mirror.

"Amy, you're gorgeous. Now get outta here so I can

get some work done!"

"Don't wait up!"

The door closed behind her and I padded to the kitchen. Some chips piled with shredded cheddar and nuked for a minute constituted trashy nachos. I grabbed a Diet Coke and piled up on the sofa, remote on one side, files on the other, and laptop on the coffee table. I flipped channels til I found a ghost hunting show that seemed appropriately trashy. Thus set up, for the next few hours I lost myself in several projects, finished Abe's spread completely, and jotted a few notes about Nancy's cocktail party. Feeling extremely gratified with what I'd accomplished, I closed my laptop and stretched out on the sofa with a fluffy throw. I checked my phone. No messages. I perused the magazine's new Facebook and Twitter accounts, very pleased with what our interns had done. They had posted sneak peeks at the upcoming issue and there were tons of positive comments and shares. I hoped that boded well for the future. I scrolled through my Facebook, stopping to make semi-clever comments on friends' posts.

My phone dinged with a message. It was Jake. My heart gave a little thump.

Jake: Whatcha doing?
Me: Watching bad TV. Don't judge.
Jake: Something you'd rather be doing?
Me: I can think of a few things…
Jake: Such as?
Me: You're making me blush.
Jake: Would I be one of those things?
Me: Maybe
Jake: Maybe?
Me: Definitely.
Jake: Good. Open the door.

What? Shit! I looked down at my baggy pink PJs and holey t-shirt. My hair was piled on top of my head, my reading glasses perched on my unmade-up face. *Yeah. Cute.* Definitely ready for company. Nothing to do but open the door. Jake was leaning against the doorframe looking sexy as hell.

"I could say I was in the neighborhood, but I'd be lying," he said. He looked me over head to toe and I just knew he had some smartass comment about my attire.

"Shush...you. Don't say it. I know. But I wasn't exactly expecting company," I said.

"Well, it's not Victoria's Secret. Then again, if it was, I'd have to wonder whom you were expecting since you didn't know I'd show up. Then I'd have put the poor sucker out of his misery. But as it is, I approve. All snuggly and kinda geeky - did I tell you about my school-girl fantasy?" He smiled and walked into the house. I backed away from him giggling. He was being so silly. He was dangerous definitely, but somehow more relaxed and carefree. I liked it.

"Well you should see my Ann of Green Gables outfit then. Uh…don't ask. It was a gift. Truthfully I'm a wreck, and there is something very very wrong with you, I think."

"Mmmmmm…you've no idea. I really need to know about the Ann outfit, but for starters, there is something wrong…"

"Oh?"

"Yeah, under those five-sizes too big PJs, I know there's a smoking hot body, and I know that behind these," he removed my reading glasses, "are the most incredible blue eyes. And what's wrong is that is you're not naked yet and my hands are not making that body sing. But I'm hoping you can help me solve that problem."

He looked at me. The need in his eyes mirrored my own. My body was already singing. He hadn't even touched me yet. He picked me up. "Which way?" he asked.

I pointed to my room and he carried me through the door, kicking it closed with his foot. He laid me on the bed and proceeded to take his shirt off. I ogled his body, hard and ripped from outdoor work, muscles flexing fluidly under sunbaked skin. I wanted to touch and taste every inch of him. I sat up on the bed. God he was beautiful.

"Take off your shirt," he commanded. My nipples, already taut, puckered more from the cool rush of air. Jake lay me back and straddled me. His mouth immediately covered one hard nipple, sucking and nipping. His hands cupped my breasts, pushing them up toward his mouth. He took one and then the other until I was writhing with that sweet ache. My hands explored his shoulders and back before sliding under his jeans to grasp his toned butt. He nipped and kissed his way down my stomach. The burn between my thighs was unbearable and my back arched to meet the bulge in his jeans. He rose up, allowing me to slide his jeans and briefs down his hips, freeing his formidable erection.

"Please. I need you. In me," I heard myself say. He pulled off my PJ bottoms with one smooth motion and kissed a line from my naval to my throbbing entrance.

"God, Mel. You are so responsive. You're killing me." He lowered his head and I felt his warm mouth take me and his tongue lapped around my clit as his fingers pinched the nerve-filled base. My world swam. The sensation of his tongue in me was overwhelming. He groaned into my apex, "I love drinking you…so sweet." I felt myself tipping over the edge of oblivion. My muscles tightened.

"Oh no you don't, baby. Not yet."

"Please, don't stop."

"Tell me what you need. Tell me what you want."

"I want you. I want this." I grabbed his dick.

He positioned himself over me and teased me with his shaft, lubricating the head in my juices. He entered me slowly, sliding through my wet folds. He looked into my eyes and straight into my soul. "You have no idea how good you feel," he said and a twist of his hips sent a shudder of pleasure through me. He angled us so that with each thrust, his pelvis rubbed my clit, intensifying my reaction. My sex clamped down on him and I lifted to push him deep to that place that set of the chain reaction of my release. The build was intolerable, painful, exquisite. Then he stilled.

"Don't you dare," I threatened him.

He smiled, "Not yet, love."

Did he really just say that? He sat back, twisted his hips, and rubbed my swollen nub with his fingers. I felt him everywhere as he rotated and teased until I couldn't take it and squirmed under him. He smiled at me. He knew exactly what he was doing to me and began to thrust deep and slow, in and out. His movements quickened and the tortuous build began again. He lowered himself to claim my mouth again.

"Please, I can't - I want, I need," I breathed into his mouth.

He pulled out slowly and then plunged deep and hard, picking up a furious pace, driving me up and over the edge. My muscles convulsed and tightened and I clenched him to me as I came hard, crying out his name. He drove into me once again and his body quaked with the force of his orgasm. We held each other tight while aftershocks vibrated through us both. We were spent.

The sun streamed through the sheers. Somewhere in the night, we had shifted so that Jake's body folded around mine like a spoon, knees folded and legs intertwined. His arm draped deliciously over my body and his hand lay just under my breast. His thumb lazily caressed my sensitive skin and my nipples puckered, wanting his touch. He wasn't even awake yet, or was he? I rolled my head slightly to find him smiling at me.

"Morning sunshine," he said.

"What time is it?" I asked. I reached over and flicked on my phone on the nightstand. "Oof, still early. Gotta go to the office today."

"Mmmmm," he pulled me back. "I could get used to this." The feel of his naked body wrapped around mine in my bed was thrilling. I wiggled a little to be a tease and gasped to find his erection hard against my rear. He grabbed my waist, pulling my hips back into position. I was already on fire for him, the dampness eager for his entrance. He pushed into me slowly and waited for my pussy to relax and take him fully.

We lay still, thus locked together. His hands splayed out against my stomach and he let his fingers lightly graze my skin, leaving goose bumps in their wake. He caressed my breasts tenderly from behind and gently tugged at my nipples until they ached. I shifted to peek at him. He smiled impishly and started to move within me. I placed my hands over his, still on my breasts. He clasped them in his and bought them down to the point of our union. I could feel him as he slid in and out of me, wet with my juices, creating those amazing tremors. Our hands, joined together, touched him and then me, our fingers separating to explore our union. It was completely erotic. He placed my hands on my mound and I continued caressing myself and him. He gripped my hips and moved faster within me. Then he stilled.

While still buried deep, he rose to his knees, lifting me to all fours in front of him. He grabbed my ass with both hands and spread me wider, circling his hips and settling deeper. He reached around my waist and massaged my clit. I was blazing with heat, my mind a whirling vortex. He slid slowly in and out, making sure I felt every hard inch of him. I was quaking with need. He grabbed my hips again and thrust into me hard. I couldn't hold out any longer. My orgasm slammed through my body. His breath caught and he stiffened, pumping into me one last time. I collapsed and he rolled us to our sides, still maintaining our connection. We lay there gasping until the world slowly returned.

"Wow," I said. "Good morning to you, too."

"It is now," he answered.

We heard the back door open and close. We looked at each other and giggled. Jake got up and pulled his jeans on. I grabbed my robe and padded down the hall to the kitchen with Jake following.

Amy raised her eyebrows. "I knew there was an extra car in our driveway. Yeah – I know just how much work you got done last night," she laughed.

"Actually, I'll have you know, I accomplished everything on my task list before company arrived."

"Ya, uh-huh. Whatever you say." She winked at us and pulled out the milk and cereal. She paused, studying the countertop, holding the milk and cereal in the air. "There better not be any man-juice on here," she quipped.

Jake laughed aloud.

"Oh my god, Amy! Can you be any more vulgar?" I was laughing so hard I had to clench my legs to keep from peeing myself.

"Well, let me see…"

"Amy! Stop. No more! I'm going to have an accident right here in the kitchen floor!"

Amy stopped for a minute. She turned to Jake. I could tell she was on a roll this morning. I shook my head at her. She smiled sweetly. "I'm sorry. Where are my manners? Good morning, Jake."

"Morning Amy," he said, still chuckling. "Is this normal for this house?"

"Oh, it can get much, much worse," she said, "but we'll try to tone it down for our guest. Just until you get used to us. Then we'll serve you pornographic cookies!" I rolled my eyes at her. I didn't feel like explaining that particular reference at the moment. It had been margarita-induced folly. June Cleaver wouldn't have approved.

"So, slut, I trust your night was successful. You appear to have a rosy glow," I teased her.

"Your grandmother would so not approve," she laughed.

"Inside joke," I told Jake.

"My night was divine. Little Italian restaurant, good wine…" She made a flourish with her arm. "And I will tell you all about it later, but I've got to shower and change so I can go to the office. My minions will be awaiting my presence!"

"And I should leave you girls to your shenanigans. I've got to pack up the trailer anyway."

Jake moved towards the door as Amy disappeared to her room.

"Are you leaving again so soon?" I asked.

"Height of show season? Yeah…no rest for the weary. This one's in Tennessee, at Brownland. It's about four hours. It's not a bad drive but we'll still leave today so the horses have a few days to settle in. Be gone all week. I'll be glad when we have one at the Horse Park again - so much easier. I will try to call, but these things get busy."

I fake pouted, "Whatever shall I do? Seriously, if anyone understands crazy horse show days - but wait a minute – I see what you just did there and don't think I don't."

"Me?" he asked.

"Uh-huh – yeah you." I smiled. "Already admitting you're not gonna call?" I rolled my eyes at him. Such romance!"

"Well – see – that gets me off the hook and out of trouble. Right?"

"Fine – then I will raise you one whiney, demanding, clingy, smothering, everything-that-I-hate…" I couldn't think of another word.

"Girlfriend?" he offered.

"Right. Ewwwww…who would want that?"

"Well, minus those descriptive words, me. If you want

to be. Labels sound silly, I think, but I know I want you and only you."

Oh! My heart did a flip-flop but my brain panicked. The fact was I wanted him. Truth was that still scared me. Despite the past couple weeks; we didn't really know each other. What if great sex and witty repartee was all there was? Was it worth taking a chance? Then again, he admitted he didn't do relationships either. Could we work this out together?

"Well - I will try to remember you while you're gone," I teased, defenses up, not acknowledging his statement.

"Hmmm - I will think of something creative. I wouldn't want you forgetting me now," he said.

"I can't wait to see what you come up with. But I am terribly busy this week. Our new issue will go to print if everything goes smoothly. It's a big deal. We have a lot riding on it. The staff is going out tonight for a little motivation. And then Nancy and I are going to go over plans for her party. You remember? You did say we could do it at your place." I decided to push him just a little to see if I could unlock the haunted house mystery. "In the event of inclement weather, would the big house be available?" I asked innocently.

His face darkened momentarily. "I'm sure it's in no condition for parties. But the lounge and barns would suffice. Knock yourself out with decorating. Can't wait to see what you girls will torture me with." He ended up teasing, but I knew the house was still off limits. There was no mistaking his discomfort, no matter how he tried to mask it. What was so wrong with that house? Maybe the employees were right. Maybe there was a poltergeist.

"You know some people say it's haunted," I pushed a little further. His mouth smiled but his eyes were distant, brooding.

"Maybe, in a way," he said softly, almost to himself, "but drop it okay? I said it's in no condition for company. Hasn't been in years."

He kissed me on my nose. “I gotta run. Holler at ya later.”

I walked him to the door and stayed til his truck disappeared around the block.

14

I met Abe, not in his office, but at his house, which was just a bit further down the drive. I found him out back, puttering around in his garden clad in khaki shorts and a Keeneland t-shirt and flip-flops.

"Nice shoes," I pointed out.

He laughed, "Not many people get to see me like this, I guess. But gardening keeps me grounded. That and the sound of the horses. You know, I didn't grow up with all of this." He swept his arm over the expanse of the farm. "My mother and father always kept a garden. Never could afford a horse, though my brother and sisters begged. Dad lost his job and took to gambling at the track – eh – you don't' want to hear an old man's stories."

"No, I do." And I meant it. I was interested in what made this powerful but kindly man tick.

"I'm just a sentimental old fool at heart," he laughed, "But don't tell the natives. Even after all this time, I think they'd still like to run me out of town. Anyway, I put myself through school, majoring in finance. Found myself with more money than I'd ever had and went nuts for a while. I woke up one day and realized I had to get out of the city."

"And the track?" I didn't know if I was overstepping boundaries. "The racehorses?"

"The horses I never had – and – I know it seems counterintuitive given my father's propensities, but somehow making a success of racing helps me forgive my dad. Making something good out of something bad I guess. My old friends thought I was nuts to give up board rooms and high finance, but I like a challenge and this place was definitely that."

How anyone could not like this man, I didn't know. He was a shark in the boardroom, but he was just a gentle man at heart. I wanted to give him a hug but that was probably overstepping boundaries.

"Let's go get some lemonade and you can show me the final copy," he said. I followed him into the big house.

The meeting went well. He loved the first segment of what would be a multi-part ad campaign and we discussed an open house when the season started. Despite the success of the farm, Abe had never participated in the impressive round of social galas that marked the beginning of racing season and I told him it was high time he did.

"I heard you might be getting back into horses yourself," Abe said.

"Hmmm…Nancy told you. She's trying to coerce me. It might be working. The filly's nice."

Abe chuckled. "Yes. She told me. I can't believe after all this time, she finally went to dinner with me. I think she still believes all those stories about my lady friends."

"And should she?" I asked.

"Darling, I'm an old man now. I'll divulge no secrets, but I was certainly no saint in my younger days. Somehow, a simpler life is just more appealing now. Then again, with Nancy, how could anyone ever get bored? She's as sharp-witted a woman as I've ever met. I admit she keeps me on my toes."

I laughed with him. "Don't I know it? I'm so happy to have her back in my life. She was great friends with my parents, you know."

"I heard. Such a small world. Here I thought I was getting a hotshot New York gal, and come to find out, we have more connections than I knew. I hear you're getting friendly with Jake Hamilton as well?"

"Nancy talks too much." I rolled my eyes. "We've seen each other a few times."

"Nancy's not the only one talking. I haven't heard Jake talk about anyone the way he talks about you."

"You and Jake run in such different circles. How do you know him so well?"

"True. Racing people and show people don't often intermingle, but I serve on some charity boards with his aunt. She's a good person. Smart. And I consider her a true friend. I helped her manage Jake's trust." I hadn't thought about Jake's money at all. My surprise must have shown.

"You didn't know?" Abe asked.

I shook my head, "I knew the farm had been in his family, but I always thought he worked just to keep it together. He kind of hinted that's why the house hadn't been fixed up." Actually, he'd never said anything about it, but I just assumed given his modest habits and hard work ethic.

"Lord, girl. You really don't know. Well, Jake's mother made sure the family's vast fortune stayed with Jake, especially after his real father died. Jake was her only child and she wanted to make sure no one outside the family got their hands on it. As for the house? Heavens, it's been preserved perfectly. Jake's aunt, Jamie, makes sure of it. Jake avoids it because of - well because of the accident of course. He's a good man. Private. Many gals want his money, land, and connections. And he doesn't trust easily. But he was dealt a tragedy at an early age, something no kid ought to have to deal with. Money and greed damn near destroyed that boy's life, but he's overcome a lot. Now I've said too much, young lady. Look what pretty company does for an old goat like me. I'm sure you have better things to do than stare at these four walls – and I have to get my tomatoes in."

"Abe, always a pleasure. I'll holler as soon as the magazine is back from the printers."

I walked down the long sidewalk to my car, thinking about what Abe had said about Jake. There was so much I didn't know. A vast fortune he didn't acknowledge, a real dad he never mentioned, and the mysterious death of his mom and what must be a stepdad? I knew his parents had died, but Abe had hinted there was more to the story. What happened to cause Jake to be so guarded?

I was about to get in my car when Derrell came out of the office. *Well that's just great.* I hadn't seen him since the gallery incident, but I couldn't avoid him forever.

"Derrell." I nodded to him and opened my door.

"Listen, Mel, I want to apologize for my behavior. I think I had too much to drink without realizing. I've thought about calling a million times but I wasn't sure you'd want to hear from me."

"Derrell, no harm done. And I'm sorry too, if anything I did led you to believe…"

"Let's just drop it, shall we? Start over?" he smiled and stuck out his hand, "Hi, I'm Derrell. And you must be Melanie."

I laughed and shook his hand. "Nice to meet you." *Whew.* He wasn't going to make this difficult.

"How's the magazine going?"

"Great, actually. Thanks."

"So listen, I was just headed to lunch. Let me treat you to make up for my bad behavior."

"Derrell, thanks. But I need to get to my office. I've been gone long enough and this is push week for us. Another time, maybe."

"Well, how about dinner then? You can't work all the

time. And you have to eat."

Ugh! Enough! This guy won't take a hint. I was just going to have to be blunt.

"Derrell, you're a nice guy, and I'm sure you mean well. But I'm kind of seeing someone, so…"

"Oh. I see. I wasn't aware. I was under the impression that you were unattached. I mean, you were alone the other night. So who's the lucky guy, anyway?"

I sighed. Some cases were harder than others. "If you must know, I've started seeing Jake Hamilton."

"After I warned you? After you saw him with those drooling fawning idiots? I thought you had more integrity."

"Well, I'm sorry you see it that way. But it is what it is." I was tired of this conversation. I turned to leave.

"Mel, wait. Listen. I'm sorry. I care about you. Just be careful. That guy is bad news for women."

"I'll take it under advisement, Derrell. Gotta run!"

Well, that was awkward. I wondered if I should tell Abe his brilliant manager and accountant was a looney toon. Poor guy was probably just lonely, but I didn't see that as my problem. And I had more important things to worry about, like finalizing our re-launch issue of the *Kentucky Equine* and getting it to the printers.

15

The office was abuzz with excitement. All the articles and layouts had been approved and were ready for press. Our small staff had pushed themselves to the limits to do in a few weeks what most publications do in a month. It had been a monumental task but they had risen to the occasion. Our editors and owners were thrilled. Due to the hard work of the staff, advertising was up by ten percent and a subscription drive boasted a fifteen percent increase. We would push for more space on local newsstands next. Now we just had to wait to see what kind of reception the re-launch issue would get from the public. As high fives and cheers went up around the office, I had an idea. A big celebratory bash might be just the thing *Kentucky Equine* needed to do. It would cost some money, but it was something we could invite all our advertisers, vendors and subscribers to. It was worth exploring. I jotted some ideas down so I wouldn't forget to bring it up at our next meeting.

We gave the staff the afternoon off to celebrate and get ready for the staff celebratory dinner.

We had reserved the private room at Dizzy's for the

party. Everyone was laughing and talking. Some had brought spouses and significant others. The magazine had sprung for a delicious buffet and wine flowed freely. Staff appreciation for work well done was absolutely necessary in my book. And this group had outdone themselves. A salsa group went room to room performing, which was an added bonus. Several of our group were enticed to try the sexy dance. Some were quite good, but we doubled over laughing at those who were less than graceful. The entire evening was a success. As the party wound down and people began to leave, several of us headed out of the room to the bar for another glass of wine before going home.

"Drinking alone, are we?"

I turned to find Derrell leering over my shoulder.

"Never a good sign for a relationship. Problems in paradise already?" he asked, his breath laden with alcohol.

My nerves fired warning signals up my arms and the hair stood on end.

"Derrell, this isn't your part of town. What are you doing here?" Something just felt off with this guy. I figured I'd play it nice and see what he was up to.

"Free country."

"True. You here with someone?"

He ran his fingers up and down my arm. "You, baby. You're alone. I'm alone. Could be the start of something great." He tried to move closer but I swiveled my stool. The people next to me were caught up in someone's joke telling and were oblivious to anything going on. Not that I wanted anyone to know. I wanted to handle Derrell with minimal embarrassment to anyone.

"Derrell. It's not gonna happen. We're friends, that's all. I thought you understood that."

He spoke so softly, it seemed he was talking to himself and I could barely hear him over the crowd. "You just don't see it yet. But you will. I got us two tickets to Baja this weekend. I'm a great judge of tan lines, baby." His hand somehow strayed to my knee and I brushed it away. Would this just end already? I was weirded out before. Now I was also majorly pissed off. He waived around some airline passes. *What the fuck?* He'd lost his ever-loving mind. He tripped and grabbed the bar to regain his balance, reeling into me before righting himself.

"Derrell, you're drunk and you need to go home."

He grabbed the back of my stool and spun me around to face him, the look on his face a mixture of menace and pleading, if such a thing was possible.

"Jesus, Derrell. Go home. You've had enough to drink. I hope you're embarrassed about this tomorrow. No actually, I almost hope for your sake you don't remember a thing, because you should be mortified."

"I could make you feel so good, baby. You're fucking beautiful, you know? Or…" he leaned in closer, "are you one of those girls who likes it a bit…rougher?"

I tried being polite but it wasn't working obviously. I'd had enough. I snuck a note to the bartender alerting him to the situation. I didn't necessarily want to get Derrell in trouble. He was Abe's right-hand man, for fuck's sake. And he was obviously knee-walking drunk and pathetic. Still, I was creeped out and this had to stop. Holding my phone under the bar, I texted Amy, who I knew was with Tom at the house.

Me: SOS
Amy: ?
Me: Can't lose this guy. Creep.
Amy: Be there in a jiff.

Thank god for Amy. If I'd driven, I would have just left, but I'd walked. On the off chance Derrell decided to have a complete break from reality, I figured why take chances.

"Still hung up on Jake? You'll see, honey. You'll come running. It's all Jake this and Jake that. Jake gets all the prizes, Jake gets the Equestrian Team bid, Jake gets the clients and Jake gets the girls. Except the one he killed. Yeah, didn't hear about that did you? Golden boy Jake got my sister pregnant. Then he wouldn't marry her. She's dead. Dead because of that rat bastard I called a friend."

I tried not to show my shock. My head swam. *What?* I didn't know if Derrell was telling the truth or not but I'd had enough. I'd process that later. I saw Amy and Tom pass the patio outside and scrambled off my stool to meet them. Derrell made a grab for my arm but tripped over the stool and missed. A bouncer appeared and grabbed him. He was so trashed he couldn't struggle much. *Jesus, what a mess.*

"What the hell, Mel?" Amy's eyes were bright with worry as we walked the few blocks to our house.

"You rhymed again. My god." I punched her in the arm, trying to shake off the tension.

"Gah. Got me. But seriously. What's up with Derrell? You didn't say that's who was after you. Damn he was drunk."

"I don't know. I mean, I don't know him that well. He just came out of nowhere and made all these comments that were just creepy. Apparently wanted me to go on some trip with him, as if I would just go away with a virtual stranger." Amy looked at me and raised her eyebrows. "Shush, Amy, I know the Jake thing happened kinda fast. My head is still spinning. But I didn't hop a plane and go away with him, either. But I mean - it's not as if Derrell knows me either. I met him at Abe's and then I thought we were friends at the gallery event – well, except for the little incident – but I thought that was over. Then I saw him at Abe's today. He asked me out, but I told him I was seeing Jake. I don't know. People are nuts."

"You're just so hot, men follow you like puppy dogs," Amy joked a little, "Wish I had that problem."

"Ahem!" Tom cleared his throat. He'd been walking along behind us, leaving us to our conversation and I'd almost forgotten he was there. "What, you want me to wag?"

"Tom, doll. I'd like to see you on a leash," Amy retorted, mischievously.

"Whoa, guys. TMI!" I laughed.

"Not a chance," he rolled his eyes.

"So Tom, you know Derrell - what's the story?" I asked.

"Look – we went to school together. Our parents ran in the same circles. Of course, we weren't the landed gentry that they were, but we were comfortable. I remember going to parties at Derrell's when I was a kid and being amazed by the opulence of that place. But that's about it. Jake hung with him far more than I did. They did the horse thing together. I never was into riding or competing. Dad just worked on their horses. I know there must have been some rivalry but they always seemed to get along. Derrell did have a twin sister and I know she and Jake were close. She hung herself in her room. Pretty much destroyed the family. They kept the details pretty hush hush, though. Derrell left for college in California right after and I hadn't seen him until he came back to work for Abe. I did know Jake was supposed to leave to train with the Equestrian Team about that time, but when all that happened, he gave it up. I guess he was pretty torn up about it all. Then he left for college and later came back to run the farm."

"Geez, that's tragic," Amy said. "I mean, for a young girl to do that I mean. Seems to happen more and more. Makes you think."

We walked in silence until we got to the house. Amy poured us some wine and we all piled on the sofas in the living room.

"Hey. Thanks guys for walking me home. I don't normally get freaked…"

"No problem. Glad we were here," Tom said. "I don't know what's up with Derrell. Since he's been back, he keeps to himself a lot. Or maybe I just haven't paid attention. I mean, I deal with him in some of my work for Abe, but I don't run into him socially. I'll have a word with Abe tomorrow maybe. He won't like that kind of behavior."

"Oh Tom, maybe wait. I mean, he *was* trashed. And who knows, maybe he just had a bad day. I don't want a big drama made out of this," I said.

"So you mentioned going to Derrell's house when you were a kid. What about Jake's? Did his parents do the social scene?" Amy asked. I was glad she did. I'd been wanting to ask, but didn't want to seem too nosy.

"It's so long ago. You know, his real dad passed when he was a baby. I think his mom entertained quite a bit until she remarried. I remember my mother didn't think much of the new husband. Said he was after her money. I was really young though and didn't understand or pay much attention. I do remember being there for a party one night…I guess it was the night they died. My parents left early. We kids had been playing Spotlight in the yard and I didn't want to leave. I remember in the car they were having one of those hush-toned grown-up conversations. The next day, they were all talking about Jake's parents being dead. I remember going with Mom to take food to his aunt's. We were ten when it happened. Someone said Jake was the one who found them. I never asked. Didn't seem right. And heck, we were little kids. I wouldn't have known what to say anyway. Always liked his aunt. Now there's a true lady."

"I haven't met her yet," I said.

"No? She's out at the farm quite a bit. Looks after things. You'd like her."

I was suddenly aware that I was exhausted. Between my relationship with Jake, the hectic pace at work, the Derrell issue and now all this information about sisters and parents and tragedies, I was simply worn out. I couldn't even finish my wine.

"Guys, I've kept ya'll from whatever ya'll were doing – and no, I don't wanna know," I laughed, "but I think I'm turning in early."

I lay in bed thinking about Jake and Derrell. Was Derrell dangerous or just troubled? Abe seemed to like him, but then Ted Bundy's friends liked him too, and look how well that turned out. Did I need to be scared of him? What happened between Derrell and Jake? I didn't think Jake harbored animosity toward Derrell and I wasn't sure he was aware how much Derrell hated him. Was it true he got Derrell's sister pregnant? Was that why he was so scared of relationships and kids? And did he really find his parents dead when he was ten? Somehow I was going to have to broach the subject with him, but I had no idea how. I wanted him to share freely with me. I didn't want to pry it out of him bit by bit. But I obviously was going to hear it somewhere, and he had to know that. What a mess. And with him away at a show, it wasn't like I could see him. And it wasn't something you really wanted to discuss on the phone. My mind raced in the dark until mercifully sleep came.

Dream man reappeared. But his face was blurry, tinged with sadness and loss, jealousy and greed, no longer a simple sexy dream guy.

16

I shoved aside thoughts of all men. I had a meeting that morning with the staff at the magazine. I was going to pitch the advertiser and customer appreciation gala idea. The cost might be a hard sell to the owners and editors, but if it worked, it could reap major rewards in the long run. I wanted it to be a big splashy affair with food, drink and music. I was also tossing around the idea that, for a fee, people could showcase their horses, but that might be hard to pull off with such short notice. Another option for the future might be a live auction of consigned horses. Or if the web site really took off, perhaps we could host online auctions. I didn't have time to flesh out all of the details, but before I put a lot of effort into it, I wanted the blessing of the owners and staff to at least explore the ideas. We had already scheduled a few open houses and cocktail parties for advertisers, and we were going to be spread thin as it was. Still, I was hoping to somehow coordinate a gala with the release of the newest issue of the magazine. We didn't have much time. Even if we couldn't do it now, it was still worth exploring.

After spending a few hours at the office making lists of items we needed to cover for the next issue, I decided the thing I needed was a horse. Winston Churchill got it right when he said there was something about the outside of a horse that was good for the inside of a man – or in this case woman. I headed to the house, called Nancy, and dug through unopened boxes to find my paddock boots and gloves. Just the prospect of sitting on a horse lightened my mood.

Nancy was waiting eagerly when I got to the barn. She had already saddled George and had Lissa in the crossties all brushed and ready. I saddled her and we walked out to the arena.

"I can't wait to see what you think of her," Nancy said.

I bitted Lissa up to lunge her. She played a bit at the end of my line, but then settled and was entirely sensible, easily trotting and cantering. After lunging her both ways, I brought her in, attached the draw reins, checked my girth and mounted. She stood nicely as I adjusted my leathers and gathered the reins. I settled myself in the saddle, getting used to the feel of her. It had been a while since I'd sat a horse and it felt wonderful. I clucked her to a walk letting her move forward into the bridle. She carried the bit lightly, her long neck arching in front of me easily. When she moved into the trot, I was blown away by the feel of this horse, her incredible hocks driving deep, propelling her forward and elevating her rolling shoulders. Ears pricked forward, she picked up momentum and the arena fell away behind her. She was no longer a beast tied to the ground, but a flying creature not tethered by gravity. The wind in my hair felt like freedom and I couldn't keep a silly grin off my face. Her muscles were working under me, her body square off all four corners and her knees were damn near hitting her chin in front of me. The power and grace of her was exhilarating and I never wanted to stop. Finally, I had to pull her down though, before she and I both overdid it. She stood proudly. Her whole demeanor seemed to say, "I'm special and I know it." Holy Hell this horse was amazing. She was born to do her job and reveled in her own abilities. I had never ridden anything like her, even with all my previous successes. My adrenalin was racing.

Nancy had pulled her horse up and was watching from the corner of the ring.

"Told you she was special, didn't I?" she said.

"Wow. I haven't ridden natural talent like that in maybe forever," I told her. "You're right. She's freaking awesome!"

"I told you. And I also told you I want her in the maturities. And your skinny little ass looks much better than mine."

"Nancy, don't be ridiculous. You've always been the most graceful rider I've ever seen. You were my idol growing up."

"Bah. You were young and I was too. But let me tell you, watching you on that mare is pure poetry. I know who the right rider is for that horse. I may be a good rider, but I'm also a smart horsewoman. It's important to be both. Anyway, I'm planning on shocking the horse world in a pair of those tight little breeches."

"Nancy, you're nuts." I shook my head. Nancy may have been in her sixties, but she had never let herself slide. She was as fit now as I'd ever remembered and always meticulously groomed. She frankly amazed me. "I just don't know that I have the time to commit. I'm awfully busy."

"Ah, yes…busy with our Mr. Jake."

"Nancy! Stop!" I was blushing.

"You know I adore him and well, you're made for each other. So Lissa here," she patted the mare's neck, "is a most excellent excuse to be here often. Consider that advantage as well."

"Nancy, you are bad. What would Mom say if she knew you were trying to be such a bad influence?" I laughed.

"Oh, I think she'd approve. Anyway, I'd never steer you in the wrong direction. And mark my words, your parents were a lot of fun back in the day. Didn't we just have some times?" She chuckled to herself. "They were very special."

"Thanks, Nance. I know they thought a lot of you, too. By the way, does your light-hearted mood have anything to do with a certain race horse breeder?"

"Hush-up child. You overstep your boundaries…" She winked at me. "But, maybe."

We washed our horses off and put away the tack. I glanced at my phone. Five messages came in while we were riding. I clicked the box and pulled them up. All five were from Derrell.

Derrell: So sorry about anything I said last night.

Well thank god. Maybe he was just insanely intoxicated. Then I read the rest.

Derrell: Hello?
Derrell: Please talk to me.
Derrell: I understand if you're mad.
Derrell: Don't do this, Mel.

Ok. That went from an apology to kind of pushy in my book. I wasn't sure how I wanted to respond. I'd have to think about that one. I didn't really want to tell him all was forgiven and I needed to make it clear that I would not tolerate that behavior from a friend - if we were to be friends. I wasn't sure I wanted to be friends anyway. Maybe just being business acquaintances was a better route with that guy.

Nancy noticed my expression.

"Spill it. Something's bothering you."

I sighed and told her about the previous night's events. "And there seems to be some pretty bad blood between

Derrell and Jake. He accused Jake of some pretty awful stuff. And I just don't know. I mean, it's not like I know Jake that well." I saw Nancy about to protest. "And neither do you really. You know he's a great coach and charming and I know you talk to him a lot but do you really know him?"

She had to admit, she didn't. Not really. "But Hon, here's what I do know. Whatever Jake may or may not have done is in the past, right? And if it's important to you, then you have to ask. I've never known you to shy away from the hard stuff. If you don't like his answer, then you have some deciding to do. But go with your instincts. Don't listen to gossip."

I nodded. She was right.

"And," she continued, "This business with Derrell. That's damn near stalker behavior. That needs to end. And frankly, Abe ought to know. It's his employee. And what if it's not just you? What if there are or have been others? It's inappropriate. And even if it's outside the workplace, it still reflects on Abe. Just sayin'."

"I know you're right. But I want to try to handle it quietly. I'm hoping it's just a misunderstanding. But I also think I need to keep it purely professional. No more trying to be friends."

"All right for now, but if it gets worse…" She looked at me seriously.

"I know. I'll let you know."

She brightened. "Well, OK then. I haven't had so much fun in I don't know when. You will be coming to ride again? I have a show coming up that I'm managing but maybe before I leave, we can play again. Lissa needs a regular schedule you know."

"You know you already had me. But if we're seriously thinking maturity, we need to get her to a good trainer soon. I'm a good rider, but someone needs to put the finishing touches on her."

"Already on it. Way ahead of you," she chuckled.

"Now I'm going to go play with George for a bit – maybe take him out to graze. I need some quality time with my boy."

"Later, Nancy."

She headed to George's stall and I got my duffle and walked the opposite direction, the soreness in my legs already appearing. God I was out of shape. Riding was going to kick my butt.

As I walked out to the parking lot, I thought about what to do about Derrell. I couldn't just ignore the texts. Well, I could if I was a real bitch. But even I wasn't that cruel.

Me: Sorry was busy. Apology accepted. Please stop texting me multiple times.

I hit 'send'. Hopefully, he'd be satisfied once he had my forgiveness. I'd done stupid stuff when drinking too.

A movement at the door of the neighboring barn caught my eye. I dropped my duffle in my car and looked again.

There was Jake, in the doorway, looking sexy as hell with that dark hair falling over one eye. He motioned to me and disappeared inside. What was he doing home? He was supposed to be in Tennessee all week. I was drawn to him like a magnet. We needed to talk, but my mind fogged when he was around. I followed him and peered in the doorway. He was leaning against a saddle rack, one jean clad leg crossed over the other, accentuating the bulge at his zipper. God I was out of control. His eyes hinted at his thoughts as they starkly roamed over my body.

"Have you been here the whole time?" I asked.

"Enough to know watching you on that horse has me rock hard."

"You're not even supposed to be home."

"Tell me you're not glad to see me."

I couldn't and he knew it. He pulled me into the feed room and grasped me close, our bodies crying out for each other. I ripped his t-shirt over his head and he lifted me onto a low shelf, pushing aside buckets and packets of supplements that went crashing to the floor. I felt his teeth on my neck and shivered with pleasure, not caring if his rough caresses left marks. I let my hands play on the hard planes of his stomach. My fingers tingled with pleasure at the feel of his skin and the soft trail of hair leading down beyond the waistband of his jeans. My fingers fumbled with his zipper until I freed him. I grasped his cock, rock hard and glorious, and stroked him until he groaned against my neck. His hands slid to the button of my jeans. I threw my arms around his neck and he lifted me. My flesh quivered where his skin met mine as he unbuttoned and left my jeans on the floor. He set me back down and let his hands roam my dark recesses while his mouth covered my breasts. I was wracked with spasms from his assault on my senses. I needed to touch him, taste him. I kissed his muscled shoulders and ran my tongue over his hard pecs until he grabbed my hair and pulled my head back to look in my eyes. His were dark, stormy and full of the lust I felt. "What are you doing to me, woman?" His lips came down on mine, his tongue demanding obedience from my mouth. He clutched the flimsy fabric of my panties. "I hope you're not attached to these," he said and I heard the lace rip. His fingers circled and teased my entrance, slipping inside and out until I was trembling uncontrollably, lost to anything but pure sensation. He dipped his hips closer, hand on his cock, teasing me with its smooth head. My hands reached for his ass, kneading the flexed muscles, pulling him closer to me, seeking to sooth the ache building inside me.

"Jake, please…"

"I love watching you like this," he said, "You're so fucking hot when you're losing control."

"I need you now Jake."

"No. I'm gonna take you against the wall. I want to watch you come apart for me."

His words had an explosive effect on me. My breath caught and my pulse raced. I wasn't sure I could take any more.

"Put your arms around my neck," he commanded.

I held on tight to his shoulders. He wrapped my legs around his waist and lifted my ass in his hands. He carried me to the wall and held me against it, the coolness a shocking contrast to the molten fire of my skin. He lowered me onto his waiting shaft. He filled me completely and then moved in a slow rhythm to make sure no part of me remained untouched by him.

"I want you to look at me when I come inside you."

Our gazes locked and he picked up the pace, thrusting up into me with undulating hips, sending me spiraling. The force of my orgasm overpowered me and my sex clenched around him in wild abandon. I cried out his name and dug my fingers into his flesh. I felt his hot breath on my neck as he drove his hips into me a final time. His glutes flexed hard and he pumped his hot release into me. I collapsed against him, spent, until he lowered me gently, not letting go until my rubbery legs found some strength to support me.

He nuzzled my hair with his lips. Slowly, my breath returned to normal and my head cleared. He reached around me and pulled some clean cloths from a drawer. He gently cleaned me and handed me my jeans. He smirked a little. "Sorry about the panties. Hope you don't mind commando."

I shook my head and peered up at him. "You're bad," I said.

He smiled a little and looked around the room.

"Hmmmm…" I said, "Think we should clean up before the employees report stray animals in the feed room?"

We straightened the room and the physical activity cleared my head. I needed to talk to him. I had so many questions. A part of me wished I could convince myself this was all an exhilarating romp and nothing more. But I couldn't seem to do that. Why did I have this reaction to Jake? He was dangerous for me. Maybe toxic. It bordered on addiction. I'd never been so out of control. And I'd never found a roller coaster ride so thrilling. But it couldn't be healthy. Aside from mind-blowing sex, I had no idea who this guy was. Either this thing had to move forward or it had to end. And I was terrified it would end. I mentally squared my shoulders. Better to get it over now. I took a deep breath.

"Jake. I need you to tell me about Derrell's sister."

He froze. His eyes narrowed and he looked at me sharply. "Who told you about that?"

"Doesn't matter. I need to know the truth. Did you or did you not get her pregnant and refuse to acknowledge it?" Ok, so subtlety wasn't my thing.

"WHAT?" He exploded. "Who the HELL told you that?" His eyes were dark with fury and I took a few steps backward. He turned around, ran his fingers through his dark hair and turned back to face me. "And why would you even believe such a thing?" The pain in his eyes cut right thru me.

"I don't want to believe it but sometimes I feel I don't really know you. No – I *know* I don't really know you."

"Don't *know* me? Obviously you don't know me at all." He shook his head slightly, his mouth set in a hard line.

"Then talk to me, Jake. Because, I…because I don't know if we should be doing this. I mean, just because you gave me my first real orgasm – well that isn't the basis for a relationship." I shrugged, unsure of what to say. Nothing was going to sound right anyway. I couldn't even explain it myself. That I was in too deep? That I didn't like feeling confused and out of control and yet I couldn't stop?

"C'mon," he said and took my hand roughly. He led

me back to the parking lot. "Drive around to my house. I'll meet you there."

What the fuck was he up to?

He walked around the back of the back of the barn and I heard his truck. I followed him to the little cottage behind the big house. He parked and got out of his truck and I followed suit. Instead of going inside, he strode to the back lawn. He paused for me to catch up and took my hand. The back lawn stretched out in lush greenness behind the cottage, blending seamlessly with the rolling pastures beyond. A small hill rose in front of a pristine pond. He led me there and motioned me to sit. He stood for a minute and then sat beside me. Neither of us spoke. Then he sighed.

"Jake, I…"

"No…" he said, "Let me do this." He closed his eyes as if struggling internally. Then he looked at me. "I'm not good at talking, Mel. You want to know why I drove back here today?"

I nodded.

"Because I can't stop thinking about you. I told you, I don't do this. I don't get involved. But I also told you I couldn't get you out of my system. I think I even used the word girlfriend." He gave me a little smile. "I had some free time, and the only thing I wanted to do was drive like a bat out of hell to catch a couple hours with you. And now I find out in the short period I'm gone, this is what you think of me? There are some things I just don't talk about. I thought I managed pretty well. I have my clients, a few friends and my aunt. It's all I ever needed, until you. I don't want to lose you. So ask. Ask whatever you want."

Wow. OK. All I really wanted to do was tell him never mind. I could tell this was painful to him. But I knew, for my own sanity, I had to press.

"Derrell's sister. And why does he hate you?" I said.

"Fine. When I was 19, my best friend in the whole world was a girl I used to show with. Her name was Ella and she was stunning. She was Derrell's twin. We talked on the phone every night, we rode together, and we hung out together when neither of us was seeing anyone. Which," he laughed wryly, "was almost always. I wasn't a shy kid really but I could count my good friends on one hand. I wasn't in love with her, well maybe a little, but it wasn't like that for her and I truly valued our friendship.

"She started sneaking around with this older guy – I thought he was an ass. He was showing with us but had already moved up out of our division. I suppose she was star struck – he took her to parties, drove fast cars and hung with a pretty fast crowd. She was infatuated. I'd heard rumors that he wasn't faithful, but she wouldn't hear it. Cut me off. Wouldn't discuss it with me anymore. Until one day she called, crying hysterically. He'd dumped her for another girl we ran with. She gave her virginity to him and he took what he wanted and threw her away. I was mad at her for not listening to me in the first place, and pretty much told her it was her own fault and to get over it. The few times she called after that, I never made time to listen to her. I was so caught up with being one of the youngest ever to be selected for the U.S. Equestrian Team that I thought I was pretty special. What an ass, right?

"Thing was, she was pregnant. Her parents didn't know. Heck they didn't even know she was seeing this guy – they never would have approved. I don't even think her brother knew she'd been sneaking out. Anyway, she showed up on my doorstep just before summer's end. She was supposed to leave for college, but how could she? I was such a jerk to her. I pretty much told her she was an idiot. Heck, it made me mad. She dumped me, her best friend, and went and got pregnant by some guy. Mel, she reached out to me and I made her feel like shit. I should have told her parents. I should have made her tell them…or someone. I should have talked to her for hours. I should have done *something*. Hell, I should never have kept that stupid secret in the first place. I should have told someone when she started sneaking around. Maybe she'd still be alive. She was my best friend, for Christ's sake, and I let her down."

Hot tears rolled down my cheeks. "Jake, you were just a kid."

"I know. Theoretically, I know. But still…"

"So you gave up the Equestrian Team."

"Yeah. Figured I didn't deserve to go. And I wasn't in a good emotional place to train anyway. But you know, it's okay. With time, and yeah, with therapy – my aunt insisted, I made peace with it. I let myself move forward. I figured she'd have kicked my ass if I didn't. She was that kind of friend."

"Are you sure you really made peace with it?"

He shrugged.

"Shit happens," I said, "But you weren't too blame you know. You didn't put a noose around her neck."

"No. I know that. She must have been far more fragile than I ever knew. I guess you never know a person as well as you think."

I looked at him pointedly. "Or at all," I said. "Sorry…that was callous. My mouth gets me in trouble."

"I love your mouth," he said.

"Jake, stop. We're talking."

He ran his fingers up and down my arm, making the hairs stand at attention.

"So Derrell…" I prompted, trying to get him talking again.

"I never knew Derrell knew she was pregnant. They weren't particularly close that way. We all competed together but Derrell never hung out, you know? He was terribly competitive but he had a temper. He liked to win. But he never wanted to put the work in. They had great horses, but he treated his animals and his grooms like shit. Ella worked her ass off and was all sunshine and light. Everyone loved her. She was always gracious no matter what. If she had a bad round, she thanked everyone anyway, patted her horse and worked harder next time. Their parents gave them everything in the way of horses, but they weren't particularly warm people. Those kids spent more time with their trainers than they did with their parents. And their parents only showed up to the big shows. They dressed the part, acted the part, and left. Ella always felt Derrell harbored a certain resentment toward her, which she didn't understand, because she didn't have a resentful bone in her body. She made mistakes sometimes, just so he could win – to keep the peace. I don't know – it's just – given her personality, I just never thought she'd, you know…"

"Kill herself?"

"Yeah. Just out of character. I always wondered if…" he said quietly, "but anyway, their parents hushed it all up pretty quick. Couldn't have a bad stain on the family name, especially with her being pregnant, I'm sure."

I wondered if Jake thought maybe Derrell had something to do with it. The thought crossed my mind. But his twin sister? Surely, a brother doesn't kill a sister. Jake didn't pursue it, though and I let it drop. He'd shared more with me in an hour than he had in the weeks we'd been seeing each other.

His hand strayed up my arm, around my shoulders, and down my neck and lightly traced the neckline of my tank. He wiped a tear from my eye with his other hand. I leaned into him and kissed him, my salty tears mixing with his heady taste. I slid out of my jeans. He watched, wide-eyed. I put my arms around his neck and scooted into his lap. He twined his fingers into my hair. The cicadas started their evening chorus as we sat beside the pond, locked together in an intimate embrace. I lifted his shirt and tossed it aside, then removed my own shirt and bra. He unzipped his jeans and I reached down to stroke his already hard cock. I rocked back a little and positioned him at my slit before settling forward again in his embrace, letting his erection slide into me. We sat connected as deeply as two people could be, holding and caressing each other tenderly, hands exploring each other's bodies, lost in our kiss. Then he moved and the feel of him overtook me. I gasped. He was so big inside me, he filled me completely. He rolled us over, removing his jeans entirely, and began a slow and steady thrust, bringing us to the brink and slowing again. He was driving us both crazy. I wrapped my legs around him, urging him deeper. Our anticipation built to a painful intensity. I needed release, but the pleasure waves kept coming. He pulled out, leaving me gasping. Then he plunged deep and I came around him, my core convulsing as he buried his head in my neck. His body shuddered over me. My hands, on his back, felt his muscles contract as his hot seed surged into me. I held him there and he made no move to break our connection. We kissed again and the sun glowed orange, setting over the pond.

We lay there by the pond until the chill night air made me shiver.

"I think I'm going to get you wet," he said.

"Again?" I asked.

"Mmmmm-hmmmm."

"You get me wet all right," I chuckled.

"I do seem to get that response from you. I like it."

His eyes twinkled mischievously as he pulled us up. We gathered our clothes and walked to the house. Jake disappeared in the bathroom.

I heard water running. "Jake, what are you doing in there?"

"Come in and find out," he called.

I found him sitting on the side of the tub naked, testing the water with his hand.

"Join me?" He reached out and I took his hand.

"Oh…you meant *really* wet," I laughed. But his naked body was no laughing matter. Long, well-muscled legs attached to that tight ass, the flat planes of his stomach, that chest…god, even his knees turned me on. And his cock, gloriously ready…already. My eyes drank him in.

The water undulated around us while Jake soaped my shoulders and back with a soft cloth.

"This was…unexpected," I said.

"Seemed like it's something they do in all those novels you girls read. Thought I'd try it for myself. So far, I like it. And the view is fantastic. I love the way the water laps against your skin. Kinda makes me want to do this…" And he lightly nipped my shoulder. Electric shocks shot through me.

"So I gave you your first orgasm?" he whispered in my ear.

I cringed. *God, I'd really told him that.*

"Don't get a big head over it," I tried to play it off.

"Oh, this head's been bigger ever since I met you." He pressed his erection against my back. "Your unintentional admission makes me so hard. I plan on being the only one to make you come. And I mean to make you come often, starting now."

I shivered.

He reached around and using the cloth, massaged slow circles on my stomach, moving back again to my neck, up and down my sides and over my shoulders and finally down to my breasts. I leaned back into him giving him better access. The feeling of water and cloth and skin set my body on fire. He slowly worked down again and paused before gently massaging my mound. He dropped the washcloth and his fingers played my folds, finding their way to my clit, teasing and releasing until I was all nerve endings and pressure points, ready to explode. I leaned back farther and tilted my head back to face him – my hands went to his damp hair and I pulled him down to me – our lips meeting, displacing droplets of water, his tongue meeting mine in hunger. I turned around and let my hands roam over his back, around to his hard chest and stomach, and finally to his engorged penis. I climbed over his legs and mounted myself on him, clenching my sex around him, knowing he could feel me stroking him from within.

"Mel…fuck…I don't know how long I'm going to last if you keep this up," he groaned. I smiled against his lips, "Hard and fast is fine with me." He held my forearms down and drove up into me – water swirling around us and over the sides of the tub. Again and again, he thrust up. I threw my hands around his neck, balancing on my feet, meeting his rhythm and grinding down onto him, feeling the build overtaking me. He crushed me to him with a final pump of his hips and we cried out together, our shudders rendering us speechless.

"Mel, I…" he started.

"Hmmm?" I murmured. I hadn't found the power of speech yet.

He kissed my damp hair as he pushed it out of my eyes. He didn't finish whatever it was he was going to say.

We lay snuggled in his bed.

"Ok," he said suddenly, "Since you don't feel we know each other well enough, ahem, tell me the most embarrassing thing you've done."

I caught his playful mood and we began telling silly stories, laughing at each other and ourselves until my stomach hurt.

"So you really sent a photo to the wrong number?" he laughed.

"Yeah. And we never did figure out who it was. Thank god there were no faces!"

We fell silent for a while, each in our own thoughts.

"Jake, what exactly did Nancy tell you about me. You never did tell me."

"Well, that might be betraying a confidence," he joked, "but no really, just stuff about you and your parents. And I know you had a relationship that didn't work out. I gather it was bad?"

"He never hit me," I said, "in case that's what you're thinking, but it was really bad in other ways. Things you don't get over right away." And I told him about my control freak, unstable ex and about the year I'd spent never knowing what would set him off or which version would be walking through the door. That I'd been relieved when it was the wall that took the punch instead of my face. That I would not – no - could not – deal with that emotional roller coaster again.

Jake looked at me seriously. "Lesser people would have stayed. You're strong. I admire that about you. You don't have to, but you work your ass off. I admire that too. I may not be good at this relationship stuff. I'm not saying I won't fuck it all up. But I promise I will never intentionally hurt you, so long as you promise to be completely honest with me."

"Deal," I said.

"And I promise to give you as many orgasms as you can handle."

He smiled broadly, proud of his own little joke. I punched him on the arm.

"I wish to god I'd kept my mouth shut. I didn't mean to tell you that. Just slipped out," I said.

"Oh no. It's out there now. No take backs."

Then he got serious again. "I've been hurt, too, you know. Women who didn't like *me*, just the *idea* of me tied to my money. So I've had this rule that I never take the same woman out more than twice. Keeps expectations low."

"But what about, you know…" I blushed. Maybe I didn't want to know.

"Sex? I was honest up front. And never at my house. And there have been a few women that I just had an understanding with."

"Oh – like booty calls?"

"That sounds a bit crass – but yeah. No expectations."

I wondered if Pam had been one of those women. She sure liked to hint that she'd known him carnally. The thought turned my stomach. I didn't ask.

We suddenly realized we were starving so Jake threw on some sweats and went to the kitchen to make sandwiches. I pulled on a t-shirt and grabbed my phone, thinking I ought to text Amy. I'd been gone since morning and I didn't want her to worry. There were twenty-five messages. One was from Amy. The rest were from Derrell. *Shit.* I thought that was done with. I didn't really want Jake to know. God knows what his reaction would be. I put my phone away. Jake came back with a big tray and set it on the bed. We sat, cross-legged, and ate our sandwiches.

"Can I ask you a difficult question?" I asked.

"More?"

"Tell me about the big house."

A dark look passed over his face. Had I pushed too far? He got up and paced at the foot of the bed.

"Jake, never mind. You don't have too."

He stopped and leaned against the dresser. "I never knew my real dad. He died when I was a baby. My mother remarried. He didn't really want me around much. I heard them arguing a lot about sending me to boarding school. I tried to stay out of his way. Anyway, one night they'd thrown a party. After it was over, Mom had put me to bed upstairs. But later I heard loud noises. I remember looking around and not being able to find them. I only vaguely recall going to the basement. There was just so much blood. That bastard killed my mother and then himself." He stopped pacing the room.

"Jake, that's the most horrible…"

"Please, no pity. I can't take that. You of all people…"

"Yeah, I know. But you were just a kid. I can't imagine."

"Yeah, well - Aunt Jamie and her therapists actually helped. But I have no desire to go in there. Just looking at it some days is hard enough, even now. Jamie thinks I should go in and face my demons or some such. I'd rather see the place burn. And now you know why I don't want kids. I wouldn't want to bring them into a world where that shit can happen."

I disagreed. Bad things could happen anywhere anytime. But I didn't want to argue the point. The whole thing was horrifying. Jesus, he found them.

"Jake, from your parents to your best friend…and you think I'm strong? I haven't gone through half that shit. You admire me? Hell, I admire you. I'd be in a gutter somewhere."

"I doubt that, Mel. You're far too tough for that."

"I can be hurt Jake. I just don't dwell. And I don't let it show."

Jake smiled suddenly and threw up his hands. "Well. There ya go. We're doomed. Or destined. Two closed off orphans. It's the stuff of novels."

We looked at each other and started giggling.

"Jake, that's not even funny!" I snorted.

"Yeah, yeah…it is," he said, "especially when you snort."

Maybe we just needed to lighten the air in the room. Sometimes humor was the best medicine, and we were laughing uncontrollably. When we caught our breath, I put my arms around him and kissed him. He held me close and buried his face in my neck, lightly planting kisses up my jawline. I sat back for a minute to rid myself of my shirt before pushing him back on the bed. I let my tongue dart a path from his chest to the waistband of his sweats. He tried to pull me back up to him, but I shook my head and smiled. Tonight I just wanted to please him. I quickly pulled off his sweats and lowered my lips to his waiting penis, already standing at attention. I lightly licked the head and delighted when it shivered - a live thing with a mind of its own. I kissed my way down the hard shaft, nuzzling my way under and taking his balls in my mouth, sucking gently.

"Mel, my god…" he groaned, his breath husky.

I continued back around the base of his erection,

replacing my lips with my hand on his full sac, while I lowered my mouth over him, sliding my lips and tongue along the ridges and veins. Jake's hands went to my hair and I heard his breath come in jagged gasps. I felt powerful, bringing him to this state of need. I sucked him in deeper, letting my tongue roam as I slid my lips up and down his cock. I took him in as far as I could and heard him groan in response. His hands roamed down to my shoulders and back to my head. He gently pressed, showing me with motion what felt good. I pressed him with my tongue and lips while one hand held him steady and the other caressed his balls. His grip in my hair tightened and his body writhed and bucked under me. I felt his cock harden even more before he was overcome with spasms that spilled his warm juice in my mouth. I swallowed, taking him into me, making him a part of me.

He pulled me up and kissed me, his eyes still hooded from his orgasm. His hands released their grasp in my hair, glided down my back and cupped the cheeks of my rear, massaging the sensitive skin. He sat up, moved me to his lap and laid me back gently, exposing my sex openly to him. I was aching for his touch, wet with desire and completely turned on. His fingers played along my crease, parting my folds and dipping inside.

"You have the most beautiful pussy," he murmured. I gasped, the intense pleasure too much as his fingers curled inside me, stroking my trembling walls and his thumb massaged my swollen clit. He inserted more fingers, stretching me and continuing to stroke my inner recesses. I moved, shifting my hips to help his fingers find that sensitive place inside. My body was tight with tension, fraught with need, craving release and I let go, no longer able to contain my orgasm. Light exploded around me and I came hard, clenching around his hand.

There were no words necessary. Jake gently pulled me to him and swept my damp hair from my face. I snuggled against him, our hearts beating in tandem. Nestled in each other's arms, we fell asleep.

I was bleary eyed and achy in a good way when the sun invaded, remembering the things we did and the amazing talks we'd had the night before. The ringing cell phone brought me closer to wakefulness. The bed shifted with Jake's weight as he cleared his throat and reached for the phone.

"Jake, here. Steve? Man, do you know what time it is?" Oh – Shit! What?"

He sat straight up, fully awake.

"Yeah – man, thanks for the heads up. Fuck. So when? I see – yeah – I'll make arrangements. No – I'm not actually there. Uh – yeah – had urgent business to attend back here," he chuckled. "No. Nothing at the barn. Right - now you got the idea. But I'll head back as soon as possible."

Jake paused and then laughed. He winked at me. "Yes, it was a very, very good night Steve. Enough. See you in a few." He clicked off his phone and swung his legs over the edge of the bed.

"Shit." He grabbed his jeans and shirt and was pulled them on quickly. "Listen, I'm sorry – I got to go."

"What happened? Was that Steve – as in my next door neighbor, as in the vet?"

"Yeah – apparently there's been a positive case of the equine virus in Tennessee now. Only one case so far but all horses at shows are quarantined there until they can be tested. At least they have a test now. The government has declared that no horses will be permitted to enter or re-enter Kentucky without a negative blood test. I need to get back and make arrangements since I have no idea how long they will have to stay. Steve said it shouldn't take more than a few days to get results back."

"I hope it's an isolated case," I said. I thought of this disease spreading and how it would affect all of us. It could be disastrous.

"Somehow I doubt it," Jake said, "but I'm just hoping I

can get our horses home. They're letting the show proceed anyway. I guess with the horses already there and unable to leave, may as well carry on. So I need to get back anyway. If I leave now, we can be schooling by noon."

I straightened his bed while he showered. I thought about joining him, but knew he had to get going. There would be plenty of time for that later. I kissed him goodbye before we left, each headed separate ways.

17

Amy was in the kitchen making coffee when I got home.

"So slut, what's up? How was Mr. Dark and Broody horse trainer last night? Everything okay? You look a little, er, messy."

"Shut up," I scolded her, "but if you must know, he's most excellent."

"In bed or out?" she laughed.

"Amy, I swear…" I rolled my eyes at her. "But on a more serious note, I guess they've found a case of the virus in Tennessee." I filled her in on what I knew and she immediately called all of her satellite offices.

"This is bad," she said. "If this thing goes south, I'm not sure what we're going to do. It'll be a huge hit. At least the state is being pro-active on this. It's a pain if you're stuck outside the borders, but at least we can keep known infected animals out."

We turned on the television and perused the morning paper to see if anyone was covering the virus but there was nothing yet. That was a good sign, but we bet it'd be all over the evening news.

At the office, the virus was all anyone was talking

about. Almost everyone on the staff was involved in the horse world in some way, and they were all worried. We'd already gotten word that a lot of shows and events had been cancelled for the upcoming weekend. With horses unable to get health papers on such short notice, owners were cancelling entries right and left. That left most of our staffers with no weekend assignments. Our editors set them to researching the virus.

Being a monthly magazine, we hadn't covered the virus because we figured the whole thing would blow over by the time we could get articles done. But this thing kept spreading, so an article in the veterinary health column about signs of the disease and another article studying the effect of the virus on the equine industry in Kentucky would be good. It was too late for the upcoming issue, which had already gone to press, but we felt it would still be timely in the next issue. Everyone got busy phoning trainers, owners, exhibitors, show managers and vets. Our editors decided to expand the scope of the research to include not just the current virus, but also the effect of any similar outbreaks in the past, with an emphasis on state and federal response. While I still wanted to plan our soiree, I wasn't sure this was an appropriate time. Plus, I hadn't found an appropriate venue yet.

Nancy called a little later. "Hey girl, listen…I'm going to head over to Jakes today to school if you want to join. My show was canceled this weekend. Entries were pulled – couldn't get their bloodwork in time. Sucks for us, but better safe than sorry."

"Nancy, I'm so sorry. Ya'll out a lot of money?"

"I'm hoping not. Still running the numbers. We're going to have to reimburse judges and officials for their expenses. Hopefully, they can get most of their airfare refunded. Fortunately, we were able to cancel the hotel and show grounds contracts. It's been a nightmare already this morning, though, and I need a break. I've got a couple more calls to make and then I think I'll head over. Come ride with me."

"I can't think of anything I'd rather do. I've got some things to finish, but nothing I can't do at home later - thank god for good internet. I'll grab lunch and meet you there this afternoon."

"Well, I feel better already," Nancy said as we cooled the horses out. Lissa had been fantastic. Her effortless athleticism was exhilarating and I thrilled at every stride she took. Even while walking her out to cool, I could feel the way her muscles slid under her skin and her well-oiled joints cushioned every step. She was a superior animal and she knew it. Her talent made her good, her attitude and heart made her great.

"I love this mare," I said.

"Good. And you'd better get in better shape. You're puffing more than she is," laughed Nancy.

"I'm afraid you're right."

"No. I'm serious. I took the liberty of entering you in the maturity."

Nancy noted my wide eyes and as I opened my mouth to protest, she shook her head and added, "It's a done deal. Don't argue. Deadline was yesterday and I had to make a decision. Anyway, I know you want to."

"Nancy, of course I want to, but I'm out of practice, out of shape and I can't afford the training."

"Already taken care of. And don't protest. I told you, you'd be doing me a favor. I've arranged for Lissa to be shipped to the trainer's. It's only a few hours away, so it shouldn't be hard for you to get there. Of course, you'll have to find another excuse to get out here to see Jake," she said, "but doesn't seem like you need an excuse anymore."

"Nancy, I swear - but if you must know, I do care

about him. Maybe more than I should."

"Take a chance sweetheart. Don't wait til you're my age to realize what you've missed. And you won't know if you don't try."

"I know. And Nancy? Thanks for making me ride. I've missed it."

"Right. Now - I know you have some spectacular custom suits that, judging just by looking, will still fit you perfectly. So go rescue them from those musty boxes and mothballs and let them air out. You're gonna need them."

"Yes ma'am!" I answered. I thought about trotting down the chute into the ring on Lissa with the crowd roaring and the music playing, the mare's excitement and mine feeding off each other and taking our performance to another level. My adrenalin surged. Hell yes, I was excited. I just hoped I would do that mare justice.

As I left the barn, I noticed movement by the big house. Knowing Jake was gone, I turned up the drive to investigate. A small white car I didn't recognize was parked outside and a small woman walked out of the house and shuffled busily on the porch. It could only be Jake's Aunt Jamie.

"Excuse me," I called out, "Do you need some help?" She was struggling with a big package that had been left on the porch and I ran over to help carry it.

"Oh Lord – these supply boxes – I don't know why they can't learn to leave them at the barn. Always bring them to the house. And here they sit until I happen along." She rolled her eyes and smiled, her green eyes sparkling. I instantly like her.

"Hi. I'm Melanie. I'm a friend of…"

"Oh heavens! Of course. I should have known. You're just as pretty as Jake said you were." She laughed at my expression. "Dear, I'm Jamie…Aunt Jamie…and Jake has told me a lot about you. *Oof.*" She set the large box in the back of her car. "Now I need a cup of tea – join me?"

"Oh I don't want to bother you."

"Nonsense – get in here." And she held open the screen door leading to the vast kitchen of the big house. It was magnificent. Entering the house was like stepping back in time. The kitchen had heart pine floors with the patina of age, white walls lined with china cabinets, a huge masonry fireplace, and a long oak table with mismatched chairs, all perfectly preserved. The appliances were fairly new, but the room itself looked like it hadn't changed in centuries.

She set a kettle on. "Nothing like fresh brewed tea. Come," she motioned through a door, "let me show you around and get to know you. I've been out of town with my girlfriends – so you and I have some catching up to do."

I was perfectly bewildered. What had Jake told her? She was so bubbly and warm I instantly adored her. And I could see where Jake got that glimpse of warmth. His shadows certainly didn't come from Aunt Jamie.

"Now this," she pointed to a fantastically large living room, "was the heart of the whole house when I was young – and that was a long time ago, too, Missy." The room was filled with antique chairs, huge mahogany armoires housing trophies, expensive looking rugs and a grand marble fireplace. "Flown in from Italy and sculpted especially for my grandfather's bride," she explained. "Isn't that just the most romantic thing?" She chuckled. "And over there is the dining hall," she said, gesturing to a room with a massive mahogany table with seating for at least 20 people – maybe more. Enormous tapestries adorned the walls and crystal chandeliers graced each end.

"Wow," I said.

"Uh-huh…and through those doors? The ball room." She sighed. "It used to be my favorite room in the whole house. Yes – my daddy and his daddy before him used to have the most lavish parties. Of course, we kids used to roller skate through here when we thought no one would catch us! Well – times have changed, I guess. I keep this old place up as best I can, but someday it'll fall to ruin if no one looks after it. Maybe they'll make it a museum. This old gal and I, we are both museum pieces." She chuckled again. The teakettle whistled from the kitchen behind us. "Ah – there's the tea!" Jamie trotted off toward the kitchen with awestruck me in tow. I'm sure my mouth was gaping at the enormity and grandeur of the house. I glimpsed a grand marble staircase and wondered if, in years past, the family women glided down those stairs in fancy gowns.

Aunt Jamie motioned for me to sit in an early American chair at the kitchen table while she pulled some antique Fostoria iced tea glasses from a cabinet. "There we go – now some ice – and do you take sugar and lemon or just sugar?" she asked. She placed a pair of Francis I teaspoons next to the glasses on a tray.

"No sugar. Unsweet is fine. "

"Nonsense, you're in the south. Well – Kentucky *is* southern you know and regardless of your years in New York, so are you, dear."

"Born in Ohio, though," I informed her.

"Bosh! You're here now, and that's what counts. Fine – only a little sugar. You need some meat on your bones anyway. Young ladies today…" she sighed. "Eh, it's a nice day. Know what? Come, let's sit on the porch." She carried the tray with our glasses and a plate of cookies through a pair of French doors to a broad screened porch. We settled into rockers with overstuffed cushions. The smell of heritage roses and large gardenias wafted through the room on the breeze. She took a drink of her tea and, finding it to her liking, nodded. "Perfect. Now…do tell me more about the girl who has my only nephew so enchanted."

Really? What had he told her? My heart did a little flip at these revelations.

"I don't know about enchanted," I said.

"Well, my nephew's not overly forthcoming," she said, "but I assume you know that. Still, I haven't seen him this happy in maybe forever. I actually caught him humming the other day! Can you imagine? Humming! Ha! The only other time he seems content when he's on a horse – or working with his students. And," she added, "I'm pretty sure I saw his truck here the other night when I believe he was supposed to be at a show with his clients."

I blushed.

"Oh, don't be embarrassed. I'm thrilled to death he's finally found someone who might put up with him. And care about him," she added.

I was still in disbelief at this conversation. I couldn't really imagine Jake humming either. "He's hard to read sometimes. There have been times I wasn't even sure he liked me," I said. "But then again, I supposed I'm not the most open person either. You're right though…I do care about him…a lot." I had no idea why I was telling Aunt Jamie this stuff. Something about her just invited trust.

"Well – he doesn't let many people in," she said. "Oh, there are plenty of women who've tried to get close to him, but so many were just after his money. Not that he ever called them twice anyway. I've worried over him so. It wouldn't be the worst thing if he didn't settle down, but he's young and life can get lonely. My husband died young so I know loneliness. Never had any interest in finding another, but I have my friends. But Jake, he doesn't socialize much. He's a doting nephew, but I shouldn't be the focus of his life. Most people think he's fairly well adjusted but I think it's going to take a very special someone to help him finally get beyond…" She paused for a moment, collecting her thoughts. "Well, he's had some traumatic experiences you know."

"He told me some of it," I said. "That's a lot of trauma for a child." Frankly, if I'd had those experiences combined with being used for my money, I'd probably hold people at bay too.

She continued, "Aside from the social issues, there are some other things he hasn't ever faced, no matter how many therapists I drug him to. This old gal for instance," she gestured at the house. "He won't use it, but he won't donate it or sell it either. Until he can walk in this house and face his demons, I don't know if he can truly heal. Somehow, he thinks that by avoiding it, he can avoid feeling. It's not healthy. Because if he can't face that, he also can't acknowledge that many happy memories were made here too…and could be again. Eventually, when I'm no longer here, it will just fall down. I don't want the same thing to happen to him."

I nodded, thinking of how I was unable to sell my parents' house either. Different circumstances, to be sure, but to me, letting go of their house would be like letting go of my childhood. All my happy memories of mom and dad were in that house. I just couldn't do it. Not yet. I realized I had some letting go to do too.

"I kind of understand," I told her. "I lost my parents tragically too. Not the same, I know, but…" I reached for my tea and took a cookie.

"Oh honey, even so, for it all to be out there in the media like it was for you…they wouldn't let you grieve in peace. Just awful. I'm glad you're riding again." Noticing my surprise, she added with a wink, "I notice more than people think around here, you know.

"I met your mother once," she said. "You're surprised? You know the horse community is an odd and tight-knit group. We served on a committee together a long time ago. She was an amazing woman. I didn't know your father but I was sorry to hear of their passing."

"Thanks," I said. "I appreciate that. I miss them a lot. Some days I still forget they're not here."

Jamie patted my hand and took another long drink of her tea. She thought for a minute.

"I don't know how much Jake told you. He tends to

gloss when he does talk about it," she continued, "but maybe I can fill in a little. His father died when he was still little – I don't think Jake even remembers him. His mother, my sister, remarried a few years later and her new husband was – was a hard man. He wasn't mean to Jake but didn't have much to do with him either. Jake told me they argued about sending him away. That part may or may not be a little boy's imagination. My sister would never have stood for that. Anyway, that man charmed his way into her life expecting, I'm sure, to get a piece of her money. He didn't know it was all tied up in trusts to protect against leeches like him.

"He was a controlling jealous man. When he couldn't get to the money, he took control of her. She was beautiful and vibrant and loved life, her friends, and her parties. He didn't. She doted on her only child. He wanted to be the center of her universe.

"One night, during a party, he got drunk. Very drunk. Caused a scene and ran the guests off. She called me crying and saying she knew she had to leave him. From what anyone can tell, she'd taken the table linens down to the basement to wash that night and somehow they scuffled. She died from a blow to the head, but there were other signs of the struggle. Jake's stepfather shot himself. They called it a murder/suicide, but our attorneys hushed it up pretty quick to avoid the scandal and protect Jake. We had connections like that. I supposed we'll never really know what happened in the basement that night. Little Jake was asleep upstairs when he heard the commotion. He found them. He's not set foot in this house since."

"I don't even know what to say. But I do think Jake was very lucky to have you," I said.

"Taking care of that little boy became my priority. It helped me get past losing my sister - taking care of her son. I love him like he was my own. He cares about you, you know. I dare say he even loves you, from the way he talks about you, though he may not show it or tell you. If you care about him, be patient with him. Since he met you, the air around him seems lighter somehow. Or maybe he's just growing up. He is a man after all – it takes them longer." She smiled broadly.

"How true that is," I laughed with her.

"Now, enough of this maudlin stuff. I hear you're doing incredible things with our venerable old magazine. Want to know a secret?" She looked positively gleeful. She got up and motioned me to follow her out to her rose beds.

"Absolutely," I answered, her childlike joy infectious.

"I'm a silent partner! Me! Well, investor really. Now, don't you tell. Jake would think it preposterous for an old lady to be making such investments when I should be thinking solid fixed income thoughts. But that's boring. Anyway, you can't take it with you, and I love my horse crazy state. I'm expecting a resounding success!"

"Well, I don't even know what to say. But your secret is safe. I am thinking about hosting an advertiser and subscriber appreciation party to celebrate the re-launch. I do hope you'll come. We don't have to tell anyone why."

"Oh, I wouldn't miss it for the world!" she gushed, "Just tell me when and where."

"We haven't set a date. I have to find a venue first. And I haven't quite found what I'm looking for yet."

She pruned a few spent stems off a beautiful deep pink rose bush, and then turned to face me, her face lit up.

"I think," she said with a twinkle, "we should do it here. Yes, right here in the big house. Just like the old days."

"But Miss Jamie, I don't think Jake…"

"Bah! It's exactly the thing. And I still control this estate so my word goes. I'll take full responsibility. It'll be good for him. And maybe I need it too. And this old gal," she gestured at the house, "needs it too. One last time. As I said, we're not getting any younger."

I was afraid Jake would be positively furious. I would

be. But she wouldn't take no for an answer. She was so excited by the prospect, she volunteered to spearhead the whole thing. I had serious doubts, but she left no room for argument.

"OK honey – I've monopolized your time enough already. I'm sure you have better things to do than hang out here with my old self. You run along. I've got phone calls to make!"

"Thanks for the afternoon," I said. "I enjoyed our visit very much."

"Honey you come visit any time. I'll have you pruning roses and drinking really sweet tea by the time we're done."

I actually looked forward to it. She gave me a huge hug and I returned it warmly.

There were eight more messages from Derrell on my phone when I got to the car. I didn't read them.

18

Amy was sobbing on the sofa when I got home. What the hell? It was as if *Invasion of the Body Snatchers* invaded Kentucky and took the bodies of everyone I knew, myself included. We were all completely out of character with more fucked up drama in several weeks than most people had in a lifetime. I sat down beside her, not knowing what to say.

"Ames, what happened?"

"It's Tom."

"What's that rat bastard done? I will fucking rip his eyes out."

"He wants to get married. Like next week. And I haven't known him very long and he says he'll leave if I don't accept. "

"What. The. Fuck. Is he on crack?"

She looked up at me slowly, a wide grin spreading on her face.

"No, not really. I was just watching Steele Magnolias. Gets me every time."

I sat there looking at her. Then I started laughing and I couldn't stop. And then she was laughing and we sat there and hooted like insane people.

"Amy, you are one fucked up chick."

"Eh, we needed a little humor. It's been entirely too intense around here lately."

"True that." Boy, she didn't even know the half of it. Between my work, my relationship with Jake, the weird texts from Derrell, and the equine virus threatening our whole community, it was enough to make a weaker person run away to an island and drown themselves in little umbrella drinks.

Amy caught her breath, "So I bought us a little Vino. Ordered pizza. Sara's on her way. All the boys are away and I thought we needed a little girl time. We are going to have fun and…" she plopped a box down on the table, "we're going to play this really bad game, Cards against Humanity."

"Oh shit. Heard about that. All right. Let's do it."

I slipped into my room to change into lounge-worthy clothes. A ripped t-shirt and yoga pants called my name. I clipped my hair up and sat on the bed to actually read my texts.

Derrell: Mel, please talk to me.
Derrell: Mel, stop ignoring me please
Derrell: what am I, chopped liver?
Derrell: Fuck you you fucking cunt
Derrell: Sorry, I didn't mean that. Mel…please call.
Derrell: If you saw my dick, you'd know I can make you feel so good.
Derrell: Are you touching yourself. I am
Derrell: God damned bitch. Talk to me.
Derrell: Why don't you like me?
Derrell: Why won't you give us a chance?
Derrell: Fucking cunt whore bitch, I will fucking make you sorry.
Derrell: Mel, I'm sorry. I don't know why I sent those things.

I clicked my phone off. I didn't want to see the rest. Derrell was either drunk, on drugs, or out of his mind. Either way, he scared me now. I was going to have to tell someone. God what a mess. The dude was seriously fucked up. I didn't respond. What was there to say anyway? I heard Sara come in so I threw my dirty clothes in the hamper and went out to join them.

We settled on the sofas and ate our pizza while watching a Real Housewives marathon.

"I don't know why they call this Real Housewives," Sara commented. "Seems to me it oughtta be Fake Housewives. I mean, is there any part of them that hasn't been nipped, tucked, botoxed, filled, stretched or plucked?"

Amy laughed, "Hell, those bitches aren't even housewives!"

"And some of them aren't even wives!" I added. "False advertising, if you ask me."

Amy was flipping through a women's magazine absentmindedly. "Oh my god. Here's an article entitled 'From Zero to Orgasm in 60 seconds'. Now who comes up with this shit?"

"Steve can make my engine purr any day," Sara said.

Amy snorted, "He must be a hell of a mechanic!"

"So how's Tom, these days, anyway?" I asked.

"Vroom! Vroom!" she laughed. "I'll be honest though, he's maybe the smartest guy I've ever dated. And we talk for hours, you know – really debate stuff. It's not just sex – I actually really like him."

"Well, Amy, that's some pretty deep stuff for you. Could you be in…loooove?" Sara teased her.

She almost blushed. "Maybe," she said.

"OK girls. I have a problem and I need some advice." I finally decided to share Derrell's texts. I passed the phone around.

"Fuck, shit, hell and damn," Amy said. "Mel, he's friggin deranged. Can you call the cops or something?"

"Amy, you're smart enough to know the answer to that. He hasn't done anything but send these messages. There are harassment laws, though. I've looked into that. Maybe I should get an attorney's opinion."

"Have you talked to Abe about it?" Sara asked.

"Not yet. And if he fired him because of me, I don't know that it would solve anything. But he probably should know. Maybe I'm not the only one."

"I'll call Tom," Amy offered. "I'm sure someone in his firm might deal with this stuff. If not, he'll surely know someone who does. I will not allow some pervert to fuck with my girlfriends! Have you told Jake?"

"Not yet. I don't know what his reaction would be. I don't want him doing something irrational."

"Well, hell, Mel. It's already irrational!"

"Amy, you just rhymed…AGAIN!"

Despite the gravity of the conversation, we all shouted with laughter.

"Who needs more wine?" I said, getting up to open another bottle. I hadn't realized how much we'd already had. "Jesus, girls. Looks like we bought a vineyard here," I said, waving my hand at all the empty bottles and feeling a little tipsy.

"There's another couple bottles we left outside. You might grab those while you're up," Amy suggested.

I set my empty glass on the bar and wobbled toward the doors. As my forehead met the glass, I bounced backward in excruciating pain. "OW! Shit, fuck, damn and hell! Amy! You cleaned the French doors again didn't you?"

Amy couldn't breathe, she was laughing so hard. "Hey, Mel, you almost fell!"

"Stop rhyming already, bitch! My head hurts. I think I have a lump."

I couldn't see Sara at first, but I could hear her laughing. She'd fallen off the couch and was holding her sides on the floor. "There's a – there's a door there…Oh stop!" she giggled.

My phone suddenly jumped and wriggled across the table, spinning wildly. I realized I'd left it on vibrate and for some reason, that phone skipping wildly across the table just added to the hilarity.

It was Jake, but I was laughing so hard I could barely stutter hello.

"'Hey, what's so funny?" His voice, low and sexy, made my breath hitch. I hiccupped.

"Just girl stuff. Need to know basis."

"Not talking about me are you?"

I nodded to Amy and Sara and mouthed the word 'Jake' as I headed to my bedroom. I touched the bump on my forehead and made a face at the girls. Then I answered Jake, "Why – have you done something funny?" I asked him.

"Not yet, but I bet I can make you giggle til you can't see straight."

"You do a lot of things that make me unable to see straight – or walk straight – or think straight," I told him.

"I'd like to be doing those things right now."

Holy… something. I'd lost my thoughts and the wine was really warm in my belly. My brain felt a bit fuzzy but Jake's suggestive words started a tingle of excitement that cut through the fog.

"I want you to imagine I'm there, touching you."

"OK," I said, playing along.

"Imagine my fingers playing with your pussy…do you feel me?"

"Oh yes." I laid back and imagined his fingers everywhere doing those magical things he did.

"I'm touching your beautiful creamy breasts, tasting your soft skin, parting your legs and seeing how wet you are for me."

I moaned softly, "And then?"

"I'm setting you on fire with my tongue. Your exquisite taste excites me and I'm growing hard with how wet you are getting."

Oh my. I closed my eyes and let my hands roam over my body, letting Jake's voice guide me. His voice was so husky; I almost came just from listening to him.

"Feel yourself. Dip your fingers inside and feel what I feel. You're so beautiful, baby."

I was panting with desire, my fingers were his and I was wet and aching for him. "Oh Jake, I want you. I want you here. I want you now. If you were here, what would you do?"

"I would touch you and ask you what felt good. I would tease you with the head of my cock until you begged, getting it wet and slowly sliding inside you, making sure you felt all of me. You'd be all tight and wet and you'd arch your back as I slowly moved in and out, asking you what feels good. I'd suckle you until you cried out my name. My cock would be pulsating inside you going deeper and deeper and you'd writhe against me, your pussy clenching me hard as you spasm."

I thought I was going to lose it. His hypnotic velvet voice driving me closer and closer to the edge as I touched myself, imagining it was Jake.

"Tell me how bad you want me baby," he said, his voice strained. I could tell from his jagged breathing that he was nearly to his climax. The erotic thought of him in a bed somewhere, stroking himself while thinking of me, slammed home my orgasm and my breath hissed through clenched teeth, my body stiff with tremors. I let my breath out. "Jake, oh..." I whispered. I heard him groan. We said nothing for a few minutes. It was all I could do to keep a grasp on my phone.

"How do you feel?" he asked. I could hear the smile in his voice.

"Ummm…wow. I can honestly say that's a first for me. Phone sex I mean. I liked it. You?"

"Not as good as if I were there. But I like that I give you firsts - first real orgasm, first phone sex. I'm looking forward to exploring more firsts with you. Maybe you could send me some photos to distract me. Nobody does to me what you do, Mel."

"Mmm…I'll work on that." I was drifting off, my body overtaken by wine and orgasm. The fog rolled in and somewhere in that fog, I knew I loved him.

"Mel?"

"Yes, Jake."

"Go take two ibuprofen and drink a big glass of water."

"Hmmmm? Why?" I mumbled.

"Because I suspect you're going to have a bit of a hangover tomorrow. I'm trying to prevent that for you."

"Thanks, you're so thoughtful."

"I try babe, I try. Now imagine I'm tucking you in. I'm kissing you on the tip of your pretty nose."

"Hmmmmm…" I mumbled. And I was out.

I should have taken the ibuprofen. I rolled over in my bed, cursing the sun streaming through my window, my head throbbing behind my eyes. I wasn't usually so irresponsible. I was going to pay the consequences today. I had to get to the office. I had things to do. I tried to sit up, but the jackhammer in my head forced me back down. I lay there a few minutes more, willing myself finally to stumble to the bathroom, rifle though a cabinet and pop two Tylenol pills down the hatch. *Water. Blessed water.* The lump on my forehead wasn't as bad as I thought. A little makeup ought to cover that.

After a shower, I felt marginally sub-human but it was an improvement. *Food.* I wrapped a towel around my head and beelined for the kitchen. Amy was already there, the smell of fabulously crispy bacon rising from her frying pan.

"Morning," I groaned. I grabbed the eggs from the fridge. Amy turned to look at me and I started laughing. Couldn't help it. "My god, you look like I feel," I said.

She knitted her brows at me. "Gee thanks. Although I

will admit… I'm afraid if I go out I'll scare old ladies, children and the socialites at Fresh Market."

I laughed and scanned the counter tops, taking note of the empty bottles, glasses and dried droplets of red wine. It looked like someone lost a knife fight and bled all over the counter. "Ugh. I don't even want to see this."

"I know, right? I smelled old wine when I came in this morning. Bout made me barf."

We looked at each other.

"So how was Jake last night? Must have been mighty good conversation since you never came back to rejoin the game."

"Sorry bout that. Well – maybe not. If I'd stuck around, no telling how much worse I'd feel this morning. I think that's two extra bottles opened that weren't when I left. And Jake's fine, by the way. Really fine. Really, really fine," I exaggerated and hugged myself.

"Just as I thought. Must have been one hell of a phone call."

"You have no idea," I said.

"Oh really? Sounded good from the living room!"

"Amy! Seriously?"

"No. But the look on your face just now was priceless. Here – have some bacon." She shoved a plate at me before I could throw something at her. "Bacon cures everything."

We ate in silence, each of us lost in our own thoughts. Amy finally pushed her plate back. "Ugh. I have to get to my office. I've had five voicemails already from the minions. Everyone is panicked about this virus. So far, only one mortality claim, but there are a few major medicals as well. All out of state clients. Nothing in Kentucky yet. I sure as hell hope this doesn't get worse."

"Did Sara mention any news from Steve? I know he's working the show horse circuit. He's the one that called Jake about the quarantined horses at the show grounds."

"Only thing I've heard is they know there's a short incubation period. And they developed a faster blood test.

So maybe Jake can get his horses home quicker than he thought. It's still turning up in random places though, and they don't know how it's spreading."

"Crap!" I said suddenly, making Amy jump.

"Jesus, Mel, I hate when you do that! You made me spill my OJ."

"Sorry. I just thought of something. Nancy was going to send the filly to the trainer's this week. I suppose there's no law against shipping horses within the state, but I'm guessing all farms will be extra careful about horses coming in and out."

"What are you even talking about?" Amy looked at me quizzically.

"Oh! I forgot to tell you…Nancy entered her filly in the maturities…and I'm riding her."

"I can't believe you forgot to tell me! I am positively pea green with envy. But I'm happy for you. Finally rejoining the show world? I miss my horse. He's probably enjoying being a lawn ornament though," she chuckled. "Still, I will absolutely take off work to cheer you on. I may even have to come watch you practice - if the filly is as good as you say."

"Oh, Amy – she is. You'll like her."

"And have you decided what to do about Derrell?"

"When the magazine issue is done, I need to run an advance copy over to Abe before the general circulation goes out, so I figured I might talk to him then."

"Well, I'd do it sooner if I were you, but whatever. I don't know why you're being wishy washy about this. It's not like you."

"I just don't want to stir up trouble if it's not necessary. And although I've come to think of Abe as a friend, he's still a major new client of the magazine, and I don't want to jeopardize that either. It means too much to me. I need this to be a success. You know, all that time in New York, and I've worked harder and brainstormed more on this magazine than any other project I've ever had."

"OK. I get it. I just want you to be safe. If it escalates, or I find him parked outside our door, I'll do something about it myself. I'm going out with Tom tonight. If it's OK with you, I'm going to tell him. He'll keep quiet and you need some advice."

"Fine. You're right. Point made. And I appreciate it. Now, I really have to get to work. I feel so much better after breakfast with my bestie."

The printers managed to stay right on schedule and had a press proof back to us within days. The entire staff went over it with a fine toothed comb, each according to his or her specialty. It was an impressive piece of work. From its heavy glossy full color cover, high quality gloss pages, and heavier stock specialty advertising spreads, the magazine was beautiful. It was informative, interesting, and visually pleasing. At least we thought so. The response it got from the readership would be the true test. We poured over it, cover to cover, proofing every line of copy. And when we finished and gave the printers permission to proceed, we cheered in the boardroom. Then everyone went to work on new assignments. We had to keep the momentum going and we could never drop our standards. Each issue had to be as important as this one, or the magazine would fail once again. No one wanted that to happen.

I thought about Jake and wondered if he'd heard anything about the blood work. I didn't know what the show schedule was or whether he might be busy so instead of calling, I sent him a text.

Me: How's the show going?

After a few minutes, my phone dinged.

Jake: Good. Mostly blue, couple red. Clients happy.

Me: results of blood test?
Jake: not yet
Me: what are you doing now?
Jake: eating hot wings
Me: spicy or mild?
Jake: hot & wet
Me: wish I was
Jake: sweating now
Me: hot, wet & sweaty? Oh my. Come home!
Jake: soon
Me: At work. Gotta run. Ttyl.

I squirmed in my chair. The effect that man had on me was sinful. I threw myself into work, researching some ideas and making phone calls for a few open houses. They were still several months away and I hoped by that time the virus mess would be cleared up. My office phone buzzed. It was Aunt Jamie.

"I didn't have your cell number, dear. Hope I'm not disturbing."

"Not at all. What's up?"

"I was wondering if I could get a list of advertisers – oh and a circulation list."

"What are you up to?"

"Well – I told you I was going to throw this party together and I never take these things lightly."

Wow. OK. She really didn't mess around. And she sounded so excited I didn't have the heart to once again voice my reservations about Jake's reaction. She had already arranged for a band, flowers, and food. She'd hired a service to thoroughly clean the house and had painters doing touch-ups. I just couldn't disappoint her.

"Jamie, my goodness! I was just tossing ideas around. I didn't expect all this – and in just a few days!"

"Honey, I told you I don't mess around. And this just makes me so happy. I'm even going dress shopping this afternoon with my girlfriends!"

"Well – we didn't even discuss a budget for this thing – I mean, I'll have to talk to my editors and the owners."

"I told you. I am one of the owners. And the budget is my concern. The magazine won't have to cough up a dime. Consider it my contribution!"

The woman was a firecracker. I hung up the phone and sat there in disbelief. Stuff like that just didn't happen. Not even in all my New York experience. But how the hell were we going to tell Jake? Turns out, we didn't have to.

19

WHAM WHAM WHAM. The door rattled on its hinges. *Jesus damn, I'm coming.* Amy was still at her office, Sara had been at teacher in-service all day and I had just emerged from a shower after riding with Nancy. I wasn't expecting anyone. What if someone was trying to break in? I grabbed a knife off the kitchen counter, not sure what I'd do with it, but it sounded good. Might make me look fiercer than I felt. The whole deal with Derrell had made me a little jumpy. I went to the door and peeked through the peephole. *Jake! What was he doing back?* My heart jumped. I hadn't talked to him yet and hadn't heard a thing about the bloodwork being back. I quickly shoved the knife behind a plant on the console table and felt myself grinning ear to ear as I threw open the door.

"Wow! This is a surprise! I'm so glad to see you. How did you get away? God I've missed you!" I stepped toward him to kiss him, but he wasn't smiling. He pushed past me and strode to the living room. I followed him, not knowing what to think.

"I arranged for someone to look after the horses." His voice was strained and he declined to sit, instead pacing the room like a caged lion. His body was tense, the veins in his neck taut. There was no doubt he was furious.

"Jake. What? Talk to me," I said.

"Why? Obviously, you don't take anything I say into consideration. Obviously, my opinion counts for nothing. I trusted you, damn it." He wasn't shouting. Just the opposite. His voice was tight and low, masking a barely contained fury. Then he slammed his fist down on the bar, making the glasses rattle. "How could you?"

I knew exactly what he was talking about. How he heard so fast I didn't know. Jamie and I had planned to talk to him together, but obviously the grapevine had gotten there before we did.

"Jake, I…we -"

"No. I don't want to hear it. I don't know what the hell you two were thinking. Aunt Jamie I get almost. She thinks it'll be therapeutic or some horse shit. But you. I thought you of all people would understand. I told you things I've never told anyone and this is what I get. I've wracked my brain trying to figure out why you would betray me like this. Unless…unless you don't care for me the way I care for you. Or maybe I was just a project for you to fix. Or maybe you thought you could get your hands on the house. Is that it? Was it all an act? Just to get to the house? You want my money while you're at it? It's all in trusts so nice try. But my heart? Well, kudos. You got me. I fell for it. You win. But don't ask me to like it. Don't ask me to be there. And you and I? We are finished. Got it?"

I stood there in stunned silence. I knew he'd be upset but he was spouting absolute nonsense. I was furious with myself and furious with Jamie. I knew it was a bad idea and I got caught up in her enthusiasm without really regarding Jake. I loved him and I had broken his heart. Then the full meaning of his words sank in. He was breaking up with me. *What? No!* My hands and face went clammy, my heart raced and my thoughts were all jumbled. I grabbed the back of the sofa for support.

"Jake, please. No. It wasn't like that. We don't have to

do it. I'll tell Jamie it's over. We'll find a different venue. No one was even supposed to know until we'd talked to you. It isn't even a done deal yet."

"Well apparently it is. You don't know my Aunt Jamie very well. Oh rest assured - she knows exactly how I feel. But how can I ever trust *you* again? No. I'm sorry. I won't do this. You just go ahead with your little soiree. But don't expect me to be there. And when it's over, I'd prefer not to have to look at you for a very long time."

His phone rang, interrupting us. He glanced at it, almost pushed the reject call button, but answered at the last minute.

"Steve. What's up man? I'm a little busy. Why what's going on?"

I could hear Steve's voice on the other end.

"What do you mean a problem? He listened for a minute and then exploded. "What the *FUCK! NO!* There must be a mistake. You know I would never… You're kidding right?" He walked to the French doors and stared out while Steve talked. "Well run some more fucking tests!" He ran his hands through his hair and sighed, "Fine, I'll be there as soon as I can."

I was afraid to approach him, knowing how angry he was with me, but he looked so confused and defeated I couldn't stand it. I approached slowly as if he were a stray animal. "What's wrong? What's going on?"

He looked at me hard for a minute then shook his head. "None of your concern. I have to go."

And with that, he brushed passed me and went down the hall and out the door without a backward glance.

I stood staring at the closed door before collapsing on the floor, my body wracked with sobs. How had I fucked up so royally? Great hot tears rolled down my face, pooling at the corners of my mouth, salty on my tongue, and dripping off my cheeks and chin. My brain was blank, numb, destroyed, defeated. I wanted to run after him, to explain, to take it back. I wanted to turn back the clock…but I couldn't. Surely when he cooled off, he'd realize how wrong he was about me. Surely he'd see that I would never, ever hurt him. Not intentionally. My brain raced in circles, searching for a clear answer but finding none. I pulled myself up the sofa, hugged my knees and buried my face in my hands.

When I finally managed to pull myself together, the clock had jumped forward several hours. I grabbed my phone, hoping for something from Jake. There were several missed messages. One was from Derrell. *Oh fuck him.* There were a couple from Jamie.

Jamie: He knows. Don't worry. I'll handle it
Jamie: I think he's headed to your place.

Little late for that warning. I dialed her number. When I heard her voice on the other end, the barely controlled tears spilled over again and my words wouldn't come.

"Melanie, is that you?" she asked.

"Oh Jamie, we shouldn't have. I think it's over for good."

"Calm down, hon. And let him calm down. I will wait him out and talk sense into him. And don't beat yourself up. This was my decision and it's my party essentially. He can't blame you because you really had nothing to do with it. I blame myself entirely for this. I should have told him right off. I made the mistake of telling a couple of friends. I guess it just spread from there."

"Thanks Jamie. But I think he's pretty set on it being final. I just…"

"You love him, dear, just as I do. He's hurt and lashing out. Trust me to make this okay."

I sniffled, her voice calming me. "Jamie, there's something else. Something's up with the horses. I want to be there to help him, but …"

"I'm sure it's alright, but I'll check on him. And Mel, I told you to have patience with him. Be strong, dear. He loves you. Hold on to that."

Sitting on my bed, I worried about Jake. Not only was he mad, he was hurt, and now something was terribly wrong with the horses and I didn't know what. My stomach was in knots and the tears kept threatening. My eyes burned. I felt drained of all energy. I lay back, willing sleep that wouldn't come. The hurt was so deep. I didn't want to feel. I wanted numbness.

The phone rang beside me. It was Sara.

"Mel, what's up? Is Jake OK?"

"Sara, we've…we've had a fight. And I know Steve called but Jake left without telling me what's going on."

"Oh Mel, I'm sorry. I know you guys will work it out."

Yeah, right. If only you knew.

I listened while Sara filled me in. Apparently, the bloodwork had come back. It was negative for the virus, but it was positive for steroids. All six of Jake's clients' horses had been drugged. Heavily. The evidence would have to be reported to USEF, the governing body of most of the show world. The use of performance enhancing drugs was highly illegal. There'd be a hearing and if Jake couldn't provide a satisfactory explanation, he'd face suspension and possibly expulsion from the show circuit both as trainer, coach and exhibitor. Plus the horses and their owners could be suspended as well. It would kill his business. And worse, it would tarnish his reputation.

"But Sara, Jake would never…"

"I know. But the evidence says otherwise. Steve's already contacted the lab to make sure the samples were correct. He drew the blood himself so he knows they were correctly labeled on his end. Even if something happened at the lab, they wouldn't admit it. And of course, retesting is of no use since the drugs would long be out of their systems by now."

"Shit," I said, "Does Tom know?"

"Tom's already talked to Steve. I guess when Jake gets the horses home, they have a meeting set up. Tom is going to represent him, but he says the evidence is pretty air tight."

My heart sank for Jake. I wanted to be there for him, but that wasn't possible now.

"Thanks, Sara. I appreciate your telling me."

"No problem. I sure hope it gets resolved. Or at least that the penalty isn't too stiff. I mean, Jake's never been in trouble before. And I really hope you two work it out. Ya'll are so cute together."

Really? We're cute? Sometimes I forgot how young Sara and Steve were.

I suppose I dozed off a bit. A gentle knock brought me to. Amy poked her head in.

"Mind if I come in?"

She sat at the end of the bed.

"You heard? All of it?" I asked.

She nodded, "Yeah, pretty much."

"I didn't mean to…and now he thinks I'm some kind of gold digger or something…and that doesn't even make sense. Like why would I fuck him just to use his house for a party? God! I told Jamie I thought he'd be mad. But I didn't expect…and he won't even let me explain. And then all this other…"

I rambled and Amy listened.

"Amy, I…."

"You love him," she said simply. "Yeah, tell me something we all don't already know. Listen, Tom and Steve just left his house and his Aunt Jamie was over there. Give it time. Let them work it out. You didn't do anything wrong."

"I feel like I betrayed his trust. I got all caught up in Jamie's excitement. And yeah, I was thinking of the magazine too. I should never put my job over my relationship. I'm an ass."

"No. You're not. You're the most loyal friend anyone could ask for. I should know. You've been putting up with my shit for years! Have a little faith."

"Thanks, Amy."

"Any time."

Sleep overcame me at last. I had no dreams at all.

20

The weekend was over. My personal life was in shambles and I was exhausted but the magazine was back from printers and I had work to do. I wanted to deliver a few advance copies to Abe and Nancy especially. They'd been so supportive. I forced myself out of bed. I couldn't wallow forever.

I was in the shower when the realization hit me. *Damn!* Jake had been with me the night he supposedly drugged the horses. They'd pulled the blood when he drove back to Tennessee. So he couldn't have done it. I needed to tell someone. And another thought crept in. If Jake hadn't done it, who hated him enough to jeopardize his horses? Some people would do anything to take out the competition, but this was extreme. It seemed like a personal attack. I tried to call Jake, but it went straight to voicemail. Either he was on the phone or he'd blocked my calls. I called Amy and left a voicemail. She could pass that information to Tom. Maybe it was useful. Even if Jake hated me, maybe I could help him beat this thing.

I called Nancy and told her I'd meet her for lunch and bring her a copy of the magazine. She understood why I might not want to meet her at the barn. She told me things were a bit tense and the employees were walking on eggshells since Jake had been home. I told Nancy we'd talk over our lunch. Oh what I wouldn't give to have my mother back. She was the first person I would have run to about all this. Even with my best friends around me, I still felt very much alone. Nancy was the closest thing I had to a mother now. I needed advice from my old mentor.

I stopped at the office to pick up the copies and headed to Abe's.

Thankfully, Derrell's car wasn't in the parking lot. I really intended to speak with Abe about all that. Abe met me at the door of his office and ushered me in. I handed him the magazine. He took a seat behind his desk and thumbed through it, examining the ads and of course, his own spread.

"Spectacular!" he exclaimed. "Congratulations. You've exceeded even my highest expectations."

"I'm glad you like it. We'll get right to work on the follow up ads for next month as well."

"Good. Good. Now what's the story on Jake's horses?"

Abe, of course, had heard some rumblings, but as he was part of the racing world and not the show crowd, he wasn't truly in the loop. I tried to fill him in.

"I know they found evidence of drugs in the horses, but it just doesn't make sense. Jake wasn't even there on the show grounds when it had to have happened. He was with me. Of course, there will be a hearing and knowing how they've been cracking down on people, it could be bad for Jake. Who would do such a thing? And only to Jake's horses?"

"Mel – if there's anything I can do, you will call, won't you? I don't have much pull in the show world, but I do have some connections."

"I appreciate it Abe. Really. And Abe…there's something else I need to tell you."

I didn't feel like explaining that Jake and I weren't together now. But I did tell him about Derrell's behavior and the weird texts I'd been getting.

He frowned. "I don't like this one bit," he said, "and I did need to know. I won't have my reputation tarnished by someone who is ruled by his dick, pardon the expression. It's unacceptable sexual harassment. If you want me to hold off making a decision, fine. But I don't care how much of a financial whiz he is, if he behaves this inappropriately, he needs to go. I can find another CPA."

His phone rang and he excused himself, stepping outside onto the patio of his office.

I glanced at his desk, noticing the calendar. Not that I was snooping, but there wasn't much else to do while waiting. Lines were drawn through a couple of days in the past week. Someone, presumably Abe, had written in 'Derrell Off'. I felt my heart beat faster. Those were the same days Jake had been home with me; the same days the horses had been drugged. Could he have? Would he have? Did he hate Jake that much? And if so, why had he waited all this time to act on it? Stalking behavior aside, hurting horses seemed extreme.

I had to tell Jake. I pulled my phone from my purse and started to dial Jakes number. It was still blocked. I would have to drive over there. I waved at Abe to let him know I couldn't wait and headed down the hall to the front door. I started to send a group text to Nancy and Amy. Maybe they could get a message to Jake. A hand on my shoulder froze me in my tracks. I whipped around.

"Derrell," I squeaked, taken by surprise.

"Snoop much?" he leered at me.

I felt a sharp prick in my side, as if stung by a bee. Turning to slap at the offending insect, my equilibrium was off and I grabbed the side of the desk. My vision blurred. *What the… I had never been allergic to bees.* The corner of the desk came at my head too fast to avoid as my knees gave way. *Ouch.* I felt something warm and wet slide down my forehead. Derrell's face loomed over me and my world went black.

I came to on what appeared to be a cot of some sort. As my eyes adjusted to the dim light of the windowless room, I could make out cinder block walls, boxes piled high in a corner, some permanent shelving with assorted tools, garden implements leaning against a wall, and what appeared to be a laundry area. It occurred to me I was in a basement. My head was throbbing and my mouth was scratchy and dry. I tried to conjure up enough saliva to lubricate my parched throat. *What was going on?* My arms and wrists burned with a tingling numbness. I tried to relieve the pressure and realized my hands were bound tight to a headboard. *What the hell?* I shifted and found that my feet were similarly bound. Bile rose to my throat in a moment of panic and I struggled against my restraints. *Calm down. Think.* I willed myself to retrace my steps. I'd been at Abe's and – Derrell - Derrell's face. That was the last thing I'd seen. But how? Why? I remembered being dizzy. Had he given me something?

"Derrell!" I shouted. I heard a chair scrape nearby. Derrell appeared next to me. He was holding a cup.

"Sorry I had to do this Mel – but you wouldn't listen. Here, I brought you some water." As much as I wanted to recoil from him, I needed that water badly. He placed a hand behind my head, lifted it slightly, and held the cup to my lips. I fought the bile that threatened to rise at his touch. My arms ached and I grimaced from the additional strain of lifting my head. Derrell tipped the cup and I drank. Some of the water escaped, causing cold rivulets to run down my chin and neck, wetting the mattress I lay on. I shivered. I was in real trouble here and I had to get my shit together.

"Derrell," I said. "I thought we were friends. Why are you doing this? What the hell are you thinking?"

"That I love you. That I'm going to make you see that you love me too." His hot breath was inches from my face. Then he straightened and moved to the end of the bed before turning to face me.

"Mel, I've loved you from the first day I saw you in Abe's office. But you only see me as a friend." He ran his fingers through his hair. "I can have any woman I want. Women want me. But you, you wouldn't see it." He stepped closer and touched my hair. "I don't want them. I want you."

Cold fingers of panic sought to take hold. I pushed them back.

"Derrell, that isn't love. *This* isn't love." I tried to gesture toward my bound hands and feet as best I could with only my head and eyes. "You don't even know me that well. You probably wouldn't like me that much if you did. I promise. And I think you only want me because you hate Jake. But you don't have to hate Jake anymore. I know what really happened to your sister. If you'd just listen to me…"

"Jake, Jake, Jake," Derrell cut me off, shaking his finger at me as if I was a bad child. "All I ever hear is how wonderful that bastard is. I had to listen to my parents rave over him." His mouth twisted in a cruel sneer. "They wanted me to be more like him. I thought they loved him because he won, so I competed. But I couldn't beat the little shit, no matter what I did. And then he had to make the Equestrian Team and everyone made a stinking big deal over him. And my stupid sister doted on him. And every girl I ever liked - liked him instead. And now you too." Derrell slammed the wall with his fist. "Well – I'm *done*! I want you to see him for what he is - an arrogant entitled prick. He never lets anyone else win. I'm done. I want you to see that I'm just as good as he is. I can make you happy. And if I can't have you, well…neither can he."

A chill swept over me with the realization of what he meant. I caught my breath. Was he threatening to kill me? My heart was beating so hard I was sure he could see it. *Think, girl, think. Fast.* I prayed somebody would find me, but how?

"Derrell," I said, lowering my voice and hoping I

sounded contrite, "Maybe I haven't given you a chance. Maybe I was blind. I didn't realize you felt that way, really. I can be so obtuse sometimes."

His expression changed. He whined, "You're just saying that because you're here. If I let you go, you'll run."

"Derrell, I swear. I've always thought you were hot. I just wouldn't cheat on Jake – or any boyfriend. That wouldn't be right. You never let me explain that. And I didn't think you were that serious. If I break it off with him, then I'd be free to be with you. But you'll have to let me break it off or I won't feel good about it. Please, Derrell. Please don't hurt me. I want to be with you."

I couldn't believe he was buying that load of crap, but in his state of mind, he was. He drew closer to the bed. My skin crawled when he caressed my leg. His hand inched under my skirt.

"Beautiful Mel. I could never hurt you."

"That's right Derrell. I see now. I see how much I've hurt you and I'm so sorry. I didn't know."

His fingertips traced my inner thigh and I used every ounce of willpower not to clamp my legs shut. If I did, he'd know I was lying. His hand reached the apex of my thighs and glided up to the waistband of my panties.

"Does that feel good baby? I've dreamed of touching you – so soft, just as I knew you would be." He lowered his head to my breast and nuzzled me through my clothes, breathing heavily. I closed my eyes and forced a small smile to stay on my lips. *No. No. No. Please don't let this be happening.* He rose up and tugged at my shirt. The weight of my body impeded his progress. He paused, considering how to remove my shirt and pulled out a pocketknife.

"It's my favorite shirt," I told him, "Please don't. This would be so much easier if you untied me. And I want to touch you." *God what am I saying? Please let this work.* He was out of his mind and my gut was churning. I couldn't wrap my mind around what was happening. Anger and terror came in waves, together and then separately. I couldn't lose control. I couldn't give in to the horror. I had to keep my head together no matter what happened.

He lifted my shirt above the swell of my breasts. His eyes drank me in. An animal noise rose from his throat. He paused, pondering the situation. To my complete surprise, he muttered to himself and untied my hands.

"Now my legs baby," I urged, trying to sound turned on, "so I can wrap them around you."

He smiled at me. "I knew you loved me," he said. "See? I can make you feel good baby." He untied my legs and began to unzip his jeans. *Oh for the love of all that's holy, think now Mel.* He dropped his jeans and climbed on top of me. As he positioned himself over me, I raised my arms as if to embrace him. This would either work or it wouldn't, but I had to try. I brought one arm around as hard as I could and hit him in the throat while I brought my knee up between his thighs. *Bull's eye.* He howled rolling to his side and falling off the bed to the floor.

"*Mother fucking cunt bitch*!" he yelled at me. I leapt off the bed to scramble for the stairs. A fist clamped on my leg in mid-step, throwing me off-balance and I went down hard, my head whipping backward into the metal frame of the cot. My world was a violent display of color but I struggled to maintain consciousness. Derrell was trying to drag me backwards by the one leg he had hold of and I felt a sharp pang in my side. A glint of steal shimmered. *The knife.* I kicked out with my other foot and felt the cartilage of his nose give under my heel.

"*My nose! You fucking whore - that was my nose!*" He grabbed his nose with one hand and I struggled to get his other hand off my leg. His grasp was an iron clamp. I tried to crawl and drag him with me but he was too heavy. He grasped the knife again. I rolled over trying to break free.

"I will end you right here. And your precious Jake can find you here just like he found his parents," he snarled at me.

Shit. Jake's basement. That's where we were. I blindly felt around the ground over my head for anything I could use as a weapon. I felt a smooth round handle. *A shovel!* I grabbed it with both hands and brought it over my head and down with all the strength I had left. The impact jolted my body as the spade end hit Derrell's sneering face. Blood spewed everywhere and he screamed in agony. Freed, I scrambled on all fours for the stairs again, eyes on the door. I heard him pulling himself up again. *Why would he not stay down!* I heard a click behind me.

At the top of the stairs, the door flew open and Jake dashed down, passing me. I heard the impact of a fist hitting pulpy flesh and turned to see Derrell fall one last time, a gun clattering to the ground beside him.

A rush of uniformed bodies tore into the room and warm arms enveloped me. I looked up to see Aunt Jamie's face, looking worried and speaking to someone. I could just make out Amy and Nancy hovering nearby, though they looked fuzzy somehow. They seemed to be talking to me or at me but I didn't understand and couldn't answer. Jake. I wanted Jake. I had seen him. Or was it all a hallucination? And then my fog cleared briefly and I saw him. He was facing away from me, staring at a corner of the basement. I sensed he was a ten-year-old boy again, finding his mother and stepfather dead in this very basement. The one he hadn't faced in all these years. He turned to look at me and I tried to meet his eyes. His worried expression scared me and I heard a whimper escape my mouth. *Was that me, making that sound?* And then he was there and his lips were on my forehead. I clutched the sleeve of his shirt.

"I'm here, Mel. It's going to be okay now."

"Jake," I whispered. And my world went dark.

21

Everything was bathed in white. I blinked, the light burning my eyes. A persistent *beep, beep, beep* pervaded the silence. Slowly, things came into focus. I moved my hand and became aware of tubes attached to me. A monitor stood nearby. Jake slept shirtless in the chair next to me. I tried to shift, to find a comfortable place, but moving sent shockwaves of pain radiating through me. I moved my free arm. My hand was clenched around something. I pulled it up and stared. Jake's shirt. I hugged it to my chest.

Jake mumbled and opened his eyes. He sat up quickly and leaned over me. "Mel? I'm here."

My cracked lips and dry throat managed a whisper. "You look like shit," I told him.

He smiled and took my hand and kissed it. His eyes were moist and he brushed away a tear.

"I thought I lost you," he said.

"Still here," I told him. "You saved me."

I held up his shirt, raising my eyebrows in question.

"You wouldn't let go when you passed out, so I just took it off," he explained.

"How long?"

"Have you been here? Two days," he said.

I pondered that for a minute and mentally took stock of my condition from my toes to my head. Satisfied that everything was in place and working, I was suddenly overcome with an overwhelming thirst. I ran my thick tongue over filmy teeth. *Ugh.*

"Toothbrush," I said hoarsely.

Jake smiled. "Absolutely," he said. He pushed the call button next to the bed.

A team of nurses, responding to Jake's page, rushed into the room. They were all beaming at me. They efficiently checked the machine, my IV drip, and my bandages. After giving me a thorough examination, they raised my bed, fluffed my pillows and bought me a blessed toothbrush. Jake brought me a warm cloth to wipe my face. I pulled my hair back with a tie. It was disgusting, but washing it in bed was out of the question. It would have to wait. At least I was feeling somewhat human again.

The doctor came in a little later. "It could have been a lot worse," she said. "You're going to be just fine. You're one tough woman. I'd like to keep you one more night for observation, but you should be able to go home tomorrow. After that, take it easy. No strenuous activity, heavy lifting or swimming. If you experience dizziness, nausea, vomiting or swelling, or redness and pain at the incision, call us immediately. Otherwise, you may have your primary care physician remove your stitches in seven days." She leaned closer, out of earshot of her staff. "I heard you kicked the snot out of the guy that did this. Good for you."

I could only make out part of her nametag. "Thanks Dr. Kathy," I told her. She smiled and handed me a water with a straw. She nodded at Jake. "Make sure she behaves now," she said. And then she left, high heels clicking on the tiled floor.

Once the examinations were over, I was allowed to

have visitors. My friends all filed in and began talking at once. I assured them I was fine. I couldn't stand the worried looks. Amy and Nancy knew that about me but poor Sara was distraught.

"Are you OK? Have you considered counseling? Are you having nightmares? Oh – how awful. Poor you," she asked, her questions coming in a jumble.

I rather wanted to bitch-slap her but I knew she was well intentioned. Amy gave her a withering look. She took a seat against the wall. I smiled at her to let her know she wasn't really in trouble. "They offered a crisis counselor," I told her, "but I'm good. I just want to see Derrell behind bars. He probably needs more counseling than I do. Sick bastard. I'm alive and strong and I just want to get out of here."

"Who the hell did do the decorating in here?" Amy asked, laughing. "Damn it, we're all here and I forgot the wine!" We all giggled, even though laughing was painful for me. Then everyone started talking at once.

"How did ya'll ever figure out where I was?" I asked.

Nancy answered, "When you never showed up for lunch, I tried your cell several times, but it went straight to voicemail so I called Abe, knowing that you had been there earlier. He thought you'd already left. Amy hadn't heard from you, so I went to the barn, thinking maybe you misunderstood and were meeting me there," she said.

"I didn't realize your car was still in my parking lot until later," Abe said.

Aunt Jamie nodded, "I had to go to the house to check the contractor's work." She glanced at Jake and they smiled at each other. I sensed somehow that they had reconciled. "Anyway," she continued, "I heard noises coming from the basement. I thought some large animal had gotten in and called Jake to send an employee over to deal with it. I stepped out to fiddle with my roses while I waited and that's when I saw a car in the woods, where the old back entrance used to be. Then Nancy came over to chat and recognized the car as Derrell's."

"We just put the pieces together," Nancy said. "What with Derrell stalking you, your car left at Abe's, and Derrell's car hidden in the woods, and noises in the house, we figured we better call the police. Jake wouldn't wait, though. He barged into the house and straight to the basement."

"He took me to the one place that would hurt you most," I said, looking at Jake, "I don't know if his obsession was more about me or you. I guess a little of both."

"I feel horrible," Abe said suddenly. "If I'd known there was bad blood there I never would have hired him. He was good at his job, but I would never forgive myself if something happened to either of you."

"Abe - you couldn't have known," Jake said. "None of us did. He and I weren't exactly friends, but I didn't know just how deep his hatred and resentment went. If I'd known, I'd have warned you."

"All I know," I said, "is that I am thankful for each and every one of you. Ya'll are the best friends anyone could ever have."

An officer arrived to take my statement. Derrell was in custody, but he would have his arraignment and bond hearing soon. The prosecutors were asking that he be denied bail, but didn't know how that would go. The prospect of Derrell on the streets terrified me.

"Assuming you do want to press charges?" the officer asked, "I sincerely hope you do."

"Absolutely," I answered. I looked at my friends. "I know this could bring unwanted publicity to everyone. I don't mind for myself, but I need to know you guys are okay with it. I just don't want him out on the street coming after me, any of you, or anyone else he might fixate on."

"He tried to rape you, Mel," Amy said. "Jail isn't good enough. They should rip his arms, legs and tongue out and use him as a fuck pillow for gorillas at the zoo."

The officer looked at her oddly. Nancy snickered. Aunt Jamie sucked in her breath and held her hand to her mouth, her eyes wide. I looked at Jake and felt a grin threatening to erupt on my face. It really hurt too much to laugh. "Please don't mind her," I told the officer, "She's under a doctor's care." With that, several giggles escaped. It felt good.

I'm not sure the officer thought we were funny. When he was done with his questions, he left his card and told us the prosecutor's office would be in touch. I knew it would be a long process, but I needed to see it through.

Tom came in just as the officer was leaving. Something nagged at the back of my mind; something I was supposed to tell him. I just couldn't put my finger on it. Pictures in my head flashed as I struggled to remember. I had tried to tell Jake but…and then it all came rushing back. *Abe's calendar.*

"Tom, Jake - Abe's calendar - the one on his desk. Look at the days Derrell took off. It's the same time Jake's horses were drugged. And Jake was with me the night it had to have happened. That's how Derrell was able to do it without anyone noticing. I was trying to reach one of you but I couldn't get Jake." He winced, knowing why. "And Derrell caught me before I had a chance to call anyone else."

"Mel, if you and Abe would be willing to testify at the USEF hearing - that information, combined with the calendar and everything else that bastard did, should be enough to get the drugging charges against Jake dropped.

Jake squeezed my hand. "I'd have gladly taken the suspension if it meant keeping you out of danger."

Finally, the nurses shooed everyone out. Jake and I

were alone.

"Mel, I'm so sorry. I overreacted and I know it. I said things to you I didn't mean and that I know aren't true. If I hadn't, maybe you wouldn't be in this hospital bed." He turned my hands over in his, clenching his teeth at the sight of the contusions on my wrists.

"Jake, our fight had nothing to do with Derrell being a dickwad. It would have happened anyway. The important thing is you're here now. And…and I know what it took for you to face that basement."

"Honestly, when I realized you were probably down there, I didn't give it a moment's thought. All I knew was if you were in trouble, I had to get to you."

"If you hadn't, I'd be dead. I didn't know he had a gun."

He buried his face in my hair. "I've lost a lot of people. I can't lose you too. Actually, I almost lost you twice. Once I pushed you away and the other, well…"

"You did warn me you'd fuck this up," I said.

He rose up and laughed out loud. "Yeah, I did say that, didn't I?"

"And Jake? The party isn't important. I hope you know that. If you want to burn the house down, after my experience, I might even help you."

"Are you sure you wouldn't like to talk to someone? It wouldn't hurt. I speak from experience you know."

"I think I'm okay. Maybe it just hasn't hit me yet. I know Derrell is sick. And I know his issue with me was maybe more complex than just a crush gone wrong. So I don't really think I'll fear monsters behind the curtains."

"Mel, don't be flip about this. I'm serious. You've had a very traumatic experience. And it was damn near fatal." Jake was so serious it almost scared me.

"Jake, I'm sorry. I know you're right. And please don't think I'm not serious. I promise if I feel like I need to, I will talk to someone. Honestly, with Derrell off the street, I feel perfectly safe – as long as he stays behind bars anyway. And I plan to do everything I can to help ensure that happens. But right now, all I want is to go home. Well…and another drink, please."

Jake crossed the room to pour more water in my cup. I smiled thinking about him worrying over me. He was so incredibly handsome. Even though every muscle in my body ached, I felt a flush of desire for this man. He saw me staring. His dark eyes flashed and he lightly ran his fingertips over a bruise on my arm, his mouth set in a hard line. "I want to kill that motherfucker for even looking at you funny."

"Jake, it's over. We're fine."

Jake nodded and took my face in his hands. He kissed my face, my hair, my neck and then his lips found mine. He kissed me gently, tenderly, and I returned his kiss, pouring all the emotions of the past few days into it. Even in my condition, I wanted him, but he pulled back. "Plenty of time for that," he said. "Right now, we focus on getting you well." I glanced at his jeans, knowing what was there. "Later," he said gruffly, "Damn it woman, the things you do to me."

"I don't know what you're talking about," I said innocently.

22

After a week of recuperation, I was more than ready to get back to my life. Usually I liked being alone quite a bit, and for the first few days, I was thankful for the rest. But I wasn't used to being idle. Being cooped up and dependent on others drove me absolutely bat-shit crazy. Amy had invited the usual crowd over for dinner and I went all OCD on the house, cleaning anything that would stand still, with Amy scolding me and warning me about overdoing it.

"Melanie Wainright! You are the worst patient ever! You have stitches for god's sake. It's just a few more days."

"Thanks, Nurse Ratchet," I teased her. "But I have to *do* something. There's only so much trash TV I can take. I've already done what work I can do from the house. And while ya'll are out and about, I'm just stuck. I can't even have sex!" I joked.

"That totally sucks for you. I'd better alert the media when you're cleared for action. They'll be reporting earthquakes in Kentucky," she laughed.

"Amy!"

"Hey…just being proactive." She ducked my flying

sponge. "By the way, you might like to know, the latest edition of your magazine is getting rave reviews. Some of my clients were talking about it."

"I've actually been nervous about it. It was truly a team effort, but I feel like I gave birth. I don't think I've ever cared about a project so much. Blood, sweat, tears, and all that. I called to check on the office earlier. Looks like they've heard good things too and our next issue is coming along nicely as well."

"Well – it's good. And you should be proud."

"Thanks, Amy."

I finished straightening and Amy took glasses and wine out to the pool just as everyone started dropping in. Seeing Jake, all tan and wet from swimming, made me more than ready to have the damnable stitches out. I wanted to lick the rivulets of water right off his legs. *My god. I've turned into a slut.* I amused myself by wearing the shortest shorts I owned and a low cut tank. I knew exactly what effect it had on him. One glance at his crotch was all I needed.

"I'm beginning to think you only like me for my body," he scolded. We were sitting at one of tables while the others were in the pool. He played absentmindedly with my knee. Or maybe it wasn't so innocent. My skin was on fire where he touched me. No one else seemed to notice the sparks flying under our table.

"Looks like Kentucky's extreme measures seemed to have halted the virus at the border," Steve told us. "Even better, the researchers are very close to creating a vaccination. It's still cropping up here and there, but we should have some reprieve soon."

"Thank God," Amy sighed. "At least most of my clients were untouched. I was pretty worried. Hey Jake, you stud, how's things at the barn?"

Jake laughed easily, used to her sense of humor by now. Tom elbowed her. "Watch who you're calling a stud babe," he pouted, and then grinned. "Or I'll have to prove a thing or two."

"That's what I'm hoping!" she giggled.

"Ahem! Things are back to normal, I'm glad to say," Jake cut in. "The horses and my clients are all fine. Tom and I presented the new evidence and USEF dropped the drugging charges, so we won't miss any shows and I'm still in business."

"Not to bring up a sore subject but I'm out of the loop on the Derrell situation. What's up with that?" Sara asked. She'd been at teacher in-service meetings and had missed most of the news.

"The judge denied bail, thank heavens," I answered. "So I guess now they'll prepare the trial. I told them I would happily testify. They found a lot of weird notebooks about Jake. Guess he'd been following his career for years just waiting for an opportunity. I also found out, that while my case was definitely the worst, he was also stalking and harassing a few other women."

"Sick bastard!" Sara said. "I'm beginning to agree with that thing Amy said in the hospital. The thing about the gorillas. Ugh, though. That's so gross I can't repeat it!"

We all laughed.

"Here's to Mel getting her stitches out tomorrow and rejoining the world." Steve raised his glass and everyone followed suit.

"And to us, for not having to watch those two fawning over each other when they think we aren't looking!" Amy said.

I blushed clear to my toes and looked at Jake. He just rolled his eyes and shook his head.

"So I have a little present for you," Jake said, grinning. We had just pulled into the drive at my house after getting my stitches out and being cleared for activity by my doctor. Jake had already mentioned a special celebration evening he had planned.

"I hope it's what I think it is," I teased, looking at him slyly. I knew he had lessons that afternoon but I was keeping him all to myself for the next few hours. I put my hand on his leg and marveled at his strong thighs. My hand moved to his crotch. "This is all I want for a present," I said. I looked up at him.

His eyes grew dark with passion. "Actually, that's not the present but…" He jumped out of the truck, took my hand and led me into the house and straight to the bedroom. He quickly shed his clothes and I marveled at his body. I didn't think I'd ever get tired of staring at him. I ran my hands over his chest, committing to memory every inch of him. He unbuttoned my blouse and bra, slipping them off before removing my jeans and panties. We stood naked, facing each other, letting our hands explore each other's bodies. I caressed his shoulders, his back, and his firm butt while he played with my breasts. He pulled me close against him. I loved the feel of his flesh on mine everywhere our bodies met. I ran my hands down his sides to his hips. He put one hand behind my neck and brought his face down to mine, kissing me hungrily. I felt his erection grow between my legs igniting the burning ache there that only he could inspire.

"Are you sure?" he asked.

I pulled us to the bed in answer. His lips scorched my skin as they blazed a trail from my neck to the apex of my thighs. His fingertips followed, creating ripples of desire. He stopped as his fingers reached the fresh scar on my side.

"Jake. Don't stop. I need you so much."

I wrapped my fingers around his cock, gently gliding my hand along its steely length. He groaned. "Mel, I want to make this last, but I need you so badly."

"Then take me now Jake."

He entered me swiftly, my body taking him willingly. Then he stilled and our eyes met. "Oh my beautiful Melanie. God I've missed the feel of you."

"Jake, I love you." The words just slipped out.

He closed his eyes and groaned, covering my mouth

with his. I drank him in, relishing the taste of him. He thrust into me and my hips rose to meet his. His hands were in my hair, his tongue dancing with mine, our bodies joined together, electricity filling the air around us. I cried out as the waves of pleasure washed over me. I felt Jake tremble and let go. It was hot, quick, and filled with all the pent up frustration we both felt. The intensity of the moment was too much and stray tears escaped my eyes. Jake kissed them off my eyes and my nose and rolled us onto our sides, still locked together. I wanted to hold him inside me forever. His hand stroked my side slowly. He closed his eyes and leaned his forehead to mine. "I love you too," he whispered.

We lay there wrapped in each other's arms until Jake finally got up. He did have appointments scheduled.

"I wish you didn't have to go."

"Ah but duty calls. Just be ready by 6:30."

"Where are we going?"

"Huh-uh. Not telling. Just be ready."

I was perusing my closet and wondering when Amy was going to be home. I was in a quandary about what to wear for this special dinner. My phone buzzed.

Amy: With Tom.
Me: Are you coming home?
Amy: Tom planned something so no.
Me: Dammit. I need help!
Amy: It'll be fine as usual. Don't worry.
Me: Fine. See you tomorrow?
Amy: Yup. See ya in the morning. Have fun tonight!

Well, so much for Amy's help. Maybe a shower would bring on the inspiration. The doorbell rang just as I turned on the water. *Gah! Why was timing always off?* I grabbed a t-shirt and shorts and went to check the peephole. Aunt Jamie was standing on my porch with an armload of parcels. *What the heck?* Jamie greeted me, her bight eyes twinkling. "I'm playing delivery," she said.

"What have you done?" I asked, amused at her merriment. I took the parcels from her.

"Oh, it's not from me. Actually, Jake said he forgot to leave these when he was here earlier. I happened to be passing through town and it was convenient." She was obviously quite tickled with herself.

"Well, thanks. Won't you come in for a minute? I have a few minutes before I have to get ready for the mystery date."

"Nope. Can't do it. Too many errands to run. Uh – groceries and such, you know." Somehow, I got the feeling she wasn't going to the grocery but she obviously didn't want to tell me what she was really up to.

"Jamie, I wanted to say, I'm sorry."

"Whatever for child?"

"Oh – the house, the party. All that. I know you were excited. And I know it caused a bit of acrimony."

"Bah! Nonsense. The house needed work anyway, party or no party. And look, it's all turned out for the best. Sometimes things work out the way they should, you know."

I nodded.

"Now, dear. I really have to run. You must promise to stop and have tea with me next week."

I promised I would and took the parcels to my room. There was a card attached.

For my precious Melanie. Please accept these gifts and be ready for a fabulous night.

I smiled. How romantic. The first box contained the most beautiful sleeveless silk shift dress I'd ever seen. It was midnight blue with tiny Swarovski crystals at the neckline and waist. The short skirt flared just slightly to show off my waist and legs. The second box held a pair of matching Jimmy Choo pumps, which must have cost a fortune. The third box contained a blushingly racy bra and matching panties. I chuckled to myself. That gift was definitely for his eyes only. I checked the time and hopped in the shower.

Jake arrived promptly at 6:30 and my jaw dropped. Jake was clad in a real suit. It was expensively cut and seemed to be made just for him. The material accentuated his physique in ways that should be illegal. He exuded power and sex. His eyes raked over me. "Perfect," he said appreciatively.

"Wow. Ummm - just wow. So you…in a suit…" My mouth was watering. I made no sense. I didn't care. He just grinned at me.

"What – didn't think I owned one? I'll have you know I only pull it out for very special occasions and for very special people."

"So where are we going to eat that warrants such fashion?" I asked. I still couldn't take my eyes off him. Ripping his clothes off and staying in would have been fine by me.

"Nope. Not telling. It's a surprise. In fact, it's such a surprise; you'll need to wear this." He held up a black length of cloth.

"You're blindfolding me?"

"Trust me?"

I nodded. "Are you getting kinky on me, Jake Hamilton?" Part of me kind of hoped so. A little thrill of anticipation fluttered around my tummy. I'd never participated in that sort of thing, even mildly, but with Jake, the prospect was enticing.

He chuckled throatily while he tied the blindfold and whispered in my ear, "Something you want to try?" His breath on my neck made my knees weak. "Maybe," I said softly. "But only with you." Even after all we'd done, I was a little embarrassed to admit it.

"Hmmm, I look forward to experimenting. But you, my dear, are distracting me." He rubbed against me and I felt just how distracted he was. "However, we can't be late for dinner. We have reservations. Later though…" he said, his voice full of promise. I shivered. He took my arm and carefully guided me to his truck and helped me in.

I tried to feel by the turns we made where we might be headed but I soon gave up, disoriented by my blindfold. Jakes hand brushed my knees. "Almost there," he said. The wheels turned a final time and the truck slowed and came to a stop. Jake helped me out and led me slowly up what seemed to be a stone path. The uneven surface was hell on my high heels and I steadied myself on his arm. This was not the path to any restaurant I recognized.

"Okay now one step up. And now another." He guided me up a couple of steps and we continued a little way on the stone path. He was chuckling to himself and I could sense other people around. The people at this restaurant had to think we were nuts.

"Jake, what are you doing?"" I asked.

"Impatient much? OK, I'm going to remove your blindfold now."

He turned me slowly and slid the blindfold off my eyes.

Before me, the big house on Jake's farm glowed warmly. Every window radiated light. Hurricane lamps lined the stone walkway to the house leading to the wide front porch. Tables decorated with votive candles and sprays of roses dotted the lawn. People milled around outdoor bars and through the windows, I saw the house full of guests. Strains of music escaped as people came and went through the French doors of the ballroom on one side of the house. Parking attendants directed the long line of cars still coming up the drive behind us. My jaw dropped.

"Jake?"

"Surprised?" he asked quietly.

"Oh. My. God. Jake?"

"Yeah. You said that already." He was openly grinning now. I could only squeeze his hand as I took in the lights and sounds of the vibrant scene. I tried to wrap my mind around it all and failed miserably. Amy and Tom, Nancy and Abe, Sara and Steve and Aunt Jamie were all standing on the porch beaming at me. Through the open front door, I recognized members of the magazine staff, major advertisers, contributors and local celebrities and politicians. There were hundreds more I didn't recognize.

"What? I thought...You didn't have to..." I had no words.

My friends all laughed. *Unbelievable.* They'd been planning this behind my back and I never caught on. Jake hugged his aunt. "This one finally convinced me it was high time this place had some happy memories – for all of us," he said. Then he turned to me again. "And you? Well, I want those happy memories to begin with you."

Still unable to speak, I threw my arms around his neck and kissed him, pouring my unspoken emotions into it. He kissed me back, his lips parting mine and time stopped. There was only the kiss.

"Ahem!" Amy said. "Get a room, for fuck's sake. Time for that later. There's a party going on!"

We broke apart but our eyes were locked. "I meant what I said. I love you, Mel."

"I love you too Jake."

He offered his arm and I took it. Together, we entered the vibrant house, alive with the sounds of music and laughter, our friends following behind.

ABOUT THE AUTHOR

Meghan Scott lives in the heart of horse country. She grew up showing horses all over the country. When not reading or writing romances, she can usually be found riding her horse or trying new wines with friends. Follow her on Facebook or Twitter for news and updates or email her at meghanscottauthor@gmail.com

CPSIA information can be obtained
at www.ICGtesting.com
Printed in the USA
LVOW04s1943200616
493366LV00049B/1471/P